Death in A Small Town

By

gay toltl kinman

This novel is a work of fiction. Names, characters, places and incidents either are the product of the author's imagination or are used fictitiously. Any resemblance to actual persons, living or dead, events, or locales is entirely coincidental.

Mysterious Women
Cover Illustration by S. A. Reilly
Manufactured/Printed in the United States of America
2011

To Mr. Billy with love

Acknowledgements:

Thanks to Dr. Lee Salamon for putting in all the commas—and more!

Prologue
Sunday Morning

"Dad?" Eric slowly pushed open the door to the family furniture store.

The only light he saw in the cavernous dark interior came from the stockroom.

The stockroom.

A tremor went through Eric. He stepped into the store, letting the large glass door ease shut, and stood, listening, then called again. But he heard only his words echo back. The store had a stale, closed up smell, and something else which he could not identify. Something not pleasant. Something that wasn't there yesterday. Something that didn't smell like furniture.

He licked his lips; they felt so dry. Suddenly, fear rose from his feet like a fog, filling his lungs.

The stockroom. Where the light was on.

Another tremor hit him as he remembered what had happened there when he was seven.

Why did that memory come to him now?

Seven, and hiding among the boxes.

Aunt Sheila.

Now the darkness felt like a blanket suffocating him.

Dread turned his walk into a shuffling movement like that of his grandfather. No, please God, not again.

Why did he feel such dread?

He thought he heard a noise. A scraping sound. He sensed the presence of another human being in the darkness.

"Dad?"

No answer.

"Dad?" he said again, louder.

Someone was in the store, he was sure of it. He stood trying to peer into the darkness. Was it someone or just his imagination? Was he hearing things? Where was his father? Upstairs in the office? No, he would have answered the phone. Besides, there was no light in the stairway.

He wanted to turn on the overhead lights, but that meant going deeper into the darkness on his left to reach the switch. Instead, he went toward the light that was on.

To the stockroom.

Finger combing his now wet, matted hair, he moved past the dark shadows of the sofas lined up like theater seats, stumbling into one.

So warm, and the smell now was gagging him; the taste of the smell tainting his mouth.

In the short hall to the stockroom, he put his hands on the walls to hold himself up as though walking through a rough riding plane. Feeling weak and ill, he reached the threshold of the room. The smell stronger now.

He was afraid of what he would see.

Then, what he dreaded seeing again, he saw.

His sight blurred for a moment and he felt dizzy. The same scene as twenty years ago. Aunt Sheila.

No.

His father. Swaying as though a gentle breeze washed the room.

The tremors started in earnest now, causing him to stagger.

Eric lunged forward, but it was more of a lurching walk. Shaking, he fumbled as he climbed onto the cracked leather chair to hold his father's body up, releasing the tension of the cord on his father's neck.

Supporting his father's body with his left arm, he strained to undo the cord with his right. But the knot held. He cried out in frustration. He couldn't untie the cord; he couldn't stop it from pulling at his father's neck again.

Fumbling in his pocket for his jackknife, he flipped open the blade. The body of his father sagged momentarily as Eric's grip loosened. The knees had no stiffness, and the legs, encased in neatly creased suit pants, bent.

Eric felt everything in his stomach coming up.

Swallowing it back, he renewed his grip on his father's body and his effort to cut the cord with the blade. He slid the blade into the knot on the pneumatic tube. He couldn't look at the face, a ghastly mask, so close to his own.

The blade severed the cord, and for a moment both bodies swayed in a macabre dance. Then the dead weight of his father's body threw him off balance and they both fell to the grey cement floor.

Untangling himself, Eric felt tears hot on his face and his throat burned. He tried again not to look at the face, but he had to. Like nothing he'd ever seen before. A mask for Halloween. But too realistic. The face purple, eyes protruding, tongue lolling, neck livid with scratches and dried blood. Clamping his mouth closed in firm determination, he slipped the blade between his father's neck and the cord. He cut it, letting the cord fall away limply.

Now his father could breathe.

Now he could breathe.

He touched his fingertips to the side of his father's neck over the stiff white collar, red tie and suit jacket. For a moment he felt a pulse. But then he realized it was only the echo of his own pounding heart, moving fast enough for both of them.

He tried for a pulse at the wrist, but the clammy skin transmitted no life, no matter how hard he pressed, no matter how hard he willed his father's heart to beat.

Eric pulled out a crumpled handkerchief and covered the grotesquely contorted features. As he stood, shaking, he noticed a rolled up sheet of white paper jutting from his father's jacket pocket. Eric gently pulled it out as though his father slept and he didn't want to wake him.

Eric tried to focus on the words. They didn't make any sense. He read them again, but the letters squirmed like snakes. Slowly he folded the paper and slid it into his khaki pants pocket with his jackknife, noticing a spot of blood on the blade before he snapped it closed.

His tears flowed and he gulped air. He didn't know what to do. He was seven years old again, but no one was there to help this time.

Eric backed away and ran out of the store.

It was 8:50 A.M.

3

Chapter 1
Monday Morning

Gilbert told me the same thing Cal had, only with more eloquence. I should handle the press. He couldn't talk now, he said through a staticky cell phone connection. Just wanted to "make sure we were on the same page," and some more managerial jargon that sent my blood pressure up because it did not bode well. In other words, "take care of it and don't mess up." That had been his original complaint to the law firm in the past, and the reason the city now had an on-site attorney, even though part-time. No other city had been offered this service. No other city had been the squeaking wheel, but then, no other city had a manager like Gilbert.

"Cal will keep you informed," he said, his voice fading on the cell phone.

Cal parting with information was not in character. I knew him much better than I knew Gilbert. Gilbert, who'd just been hired on the rebound when the city council's first choice was arrested in a men's room in Mirasol park in criminally close contact with another man.

Cal and I went back a long way. We'd gone to high school at the same time. But then I'd gone to high school with a lot of people who still lived here. It was a small town.

Looked like I had the ball and everyone was behind me. Way behind. I didn't like walking into a situation I knew nothing about. At least it wasn't one where I was going to get shot with bullets, just with words. Here, in Mirasol, I should feel a little more comfortable. This was the town I grew up in. I knew everyone. I knew everyone's past relationships with each other.

My office was on the second floor. I took the stairs down to Cal's. "I just talked with Gilbert—" I said as I walked in.

Cal handed me a folder. I knew what it was: the preliminary

coroner's report from Dr. Delbert Webster. Dr. Del.

I sat down. I'd seen enough coroners' reports in my ten years in the district attorney's office to last me for the rest of my lifetime. For a moment I couldn't open it. Then I did. Colored Polaroid pictures of Loren's body. Colored photos are so detailed. The dried blood in lines on his throat...

I realized I wasn't ready for this. It was too close to Nate's death. And Ted's.

But those thoughts went back into their respective boxes in my mind as the professional in me assumed command.

I read from the report, "A well-nourished white male. I just can't believe he committed suicide."

"No one ever believes someone they know would do it," Cal said, picking up his coffee cup.

"You're sure it's suicide?" I looked at him with what I hoped was a stern demeanor that said something like, "Don't mess with me now."

"Yep. Who knows what lurks in the minds and hearts of others?" Cal said, hiking his dark gabardine pants up. They slipped down over his stomach almost immediately. He had dispensed with his jacket for the moment.

I looked at the pages again. All that was left of someone we knew. "I talked to him at the chamber mixer on Friday. Loren was eating a piece of cheese." I felt the paper between my fingers. "Don't suppose there's any chance—"

"—that it wasn't suicide? Nope. Lose that idea, Jo. Seen a lot of suicides and this one fits the pattern." He closed a file folder on his desk. Dismissed.

"Committing suicide is so out of character for him. When I talked to him, he wasn't...." Wasn't what? I couldn't think of how to describe Loren that night. He wasn't desperate about anything; he wasn't babbling about suicide, he wasn't—

"Hey, Jo," Cal snapped his fingers. "I was there, too. So were a lot of other people who talked to him. Just because you talked to him and he didn't tell you doesn't mean he wasn't thinking about doing it." His eyes narrowed as he glared at me to make his point, spacing his words. "Even while he was talking to you."

I pictured the scene of talking with Loren while all the time he was thinking about committing suicide. He was looking into my eyes and thinking about dying.

"But he was making plans for the future." Would I go to a mixer two nights before I decided to do it? I don't think so." Aren't suicides supposed to be too depressed to make plans anymore?" Only plans on how to do it.

"What kind of plans?" Cal said looking at me, almost interested.

"The Historical Society. He wanted to give—" and then I realized what that meant.

"He wanted to give some things to the Historical Society? Getting rid of things because he didn't need them anymore? You've just made my point, Jo."

Damn, he was right.

"But why, Cal? What was his motivation? That's what I can't understand."

"Doesn't matter—he's dead." Cal moved some papers around. His blue eyes were dark, almost black, which meant he had slipped into a not-so-good mood. Join the club, Cal.

Maybe he had the right attitude.

Taking a deep breath, I said, striving to be professional, "Give me whatever else you have."

I couldn't change how I felt. I was shaken. Loren was the last person I would have fingered as a suicide. I felt shocked and hurt that he did it. I talked with him and I had no clue as to how he felt.

Why hadn't he said something? Would I have been able to say something that cheered him up? Was he too committed at that point? But why did he go to the mixer? It couldn't have been a cry for help unless he told someone. I'd have to find that out. Was it to say goodbye to everyone? I didn't get that feeling either.

I went over the scene of Friday night again, what Loren said, how he said it, what I said, what I could have said.

And didn't.

"I just can't get over Loren committing suicide." Too much death in my life recently. Nate. Ted. Now Loren. Three people in my life who should not have died this soon. Does it come in threes? Was tragedy, for me, over for a while?

"It's a done deed. You don't need to do anything, just review the reports, keep informed, handle the press. That's it. Understand?

6

I'm supervising the case."

Why was I even trying to talk to him as a friend? He was in his police mode. All else be damned. Me, I couldn't switch roles like that. Maybe that's why I'm not a cop and he is. I slammed the file closed, stomped out, and walked up the stairs to my office to be alone with my thoughts.

I sat there for a while, staring out at the mountains and thinking about Loren. He betrayed us. He played false. He pretended everything was normal. And all the time he was planning...

No. Wait. He looked a little excited that night. Happy almost. Happy because he looked forward to doing himself in? Getting out of whatever mental pain he had? I sensed nothing at the time but bonhomie from him, the way he usually was. Nothing different, nothing unusual. Yet he did the unusual.

Enough.

I dealt out the mail. Audrey, who worked both the city attorney's office and the city clerk's office, opened it. I hadn't been on the job long and I wanted to look at everything to learn what legal cases were going on in the city. Trip and fall. Real estate negotiations. Contracts. No criminal work. Exactly the reason I had wanted the job.

Audrey kidded me that for every piece of mail I took, I gave her six. Seven today, and added two pink telephone messages to her pile. Take that, Audrey.

"Coffee?"

I jumped, sweeping my yellow pad and felt-tip pen to the floor. Audrey. The belt of her hausfrau dress rested somewhere in the vicinity of where her waist should be, an appearance belying her efficiency. She held up the pot.

I looked in my cup. A dried encrustation from Friday. I leaned closer. The body of a dead fly spread-eagled in the mess. My stomach swirled.

"No." I did want more caffeine. Suddenly, Quon Lee came to mind. "The city manager wants us to be kept apprised of everything relating to Loren Balfour's death."

"Rumor has it that Win might file a wrongful death action," she said.

Ah, more light dawns. Not just handing the press because of the suicide, but handling the press because of the wrongful death action. A civil lawsuit. "His wife? Over Loren's suicide?"

"People are saying the city drove him to it."

"People are saying? He only died yesterday," I said.

"Word travels fast in this small town."

"Just rumor, or has Win told anyone specifically?"

"Rumor is all I've heard. This might get the Main Street Project rolling." Audrey said as she set the full coffee pot on a yellow pad at the end of the conference table that served as my desk.

"What do you mean?"

"He stopped it cold. A legal stay. I'll get you the files," Audrey said.

"A stay? Why?"

Audrey shrugged. "He didn't want his store torn down, I guess."

We were silent for a moment, me thinking about the actual wrecking ball hitting the store that was almost a landmark in the town, as familiar to everyone as their own home.

"Quon Lee's is one of the businesses in the Main Street Project?"

"Right."

"I'm going to talk to him." He'd give me information that wasn't in the files. And coffee in a clean cup.

Audrey didn't say anything for a moment, just bent her head. "Why did he do it, Jo? Such a gentle man. Did you know I went to school with Missy?" His daughter. "He was just in here last week. Always so nice."

"Did he seem upset?" I sounded like a prosecuting attorney again.

"No, same as always, polite, gentlemanly." She paused, her eyes glistened. "Nobody can believe it. Nobody." She shook her head slowly, picked up the coffee pot, walked to the door, then pulled it closed on her tears.

I stared after her for a moment, thinking again about Loren. He had a round face, white hair. Handsome really. Involved in Mirasol—president of several organizations, on boards of others. The store he'd inherited from his father went back as far as the city did, almost one hundred years.

In the crush of the chamber mixer, he had been eating from a small paper plate of white and yellow cubes of cheese skewered with colored toothpicks.

"Hi, Jo, haven't seen you for ages. How's everything?" he had said.

"Loren, good to see you." A part of me had wanted to call him Mr. Balfour as I had until I reached adulthood. My parents had bought a new sofa from his store when I was a child holding onto my father's hand. "Everything's wonderful."

"Heard about your new job. Want to come in to talk to you about the Main Street Project. Glad you're here. We need you." He munched on a cube, nodding as though to emphasize his agreement with what he was saying.

"And how's everything with you?"

"Good, good. Couldn't be better. At least it will be. I know you and I will be able to see eye to eye on this." Nodding again. Smiling big time. His cheeks were reddish. At the time I thought from the wine and the heat of the room, but maybe not. "Are you still with the Historical Society? I've got some things—"

I snapped back to the present, still seeing Loren before me.

That was it!

That was what was bothering me.

He wanted to talk to me about the Main Street Project. Something in the future.

But what if he'd thought it was hopeless even to talk to me and gave up?

Then I picked up my guilt and started on a journey that I didn't want to take.

Chapter 2
Monday 11 A.M.

I spotted Quon Lee sitting under one of his five umbrella tables eating during the short lull between coffee break and lunch.

"Can I join you?"

"Youwa coffee?"

"That's one of the reasons I'm here."

I settled into the metal chair softened by a removable flower-patterned covered cushion.

The diner hadn't changed. It had been the same as long as I could remember. He had found the winning business combination—good food, plenty of it, and low prices. Quon Lee hadn't changed either.

Trees along Nutwood, the street that intersected Main at the traffic light, were old and large, shading a good portion of Quon Lee's property. For a moment, I slipped into the comfort of the friendly and familiar, being home again. But glancing at the side of the Balfour Furniture Store brought the memory of those colored pictures back again.

He returned in a few moments and set a porcelain cup and saucer before me on the paint-chipped round metal table.

Only certain people got the porcelain. Cal got one, the city manager didn't, the chief of police did, the mayor didn't, and only three of the five city council members did. And Tom, the City Hall janitor, did.

I picked up the cup, steam rising from the apple blossoms hand painted on the inside and out.

"What's new?" he said, and then before I could answer he said, "Chinese New Year." He laughed at his own joke. I had to laugh, too. "Very good meeting we had last time. Going to be good festival."

The Chinese New Year Festival was scheduled for next February. We had started planning last month. "You're the chairman—it should be."

He acknowledged my compliment, actually the truth, with a slight movement of his hand as though waving away cigarette smoke. He went back to his paper plate holding a hamburger patty, French fries and rice.

I sipped from the apple blossoms, smelling the fragrance of the coffee. The taste held the promise of the aroma. We sat without speaking for a few minutes.

"What other reason you come?" he said. His face looked like it had been designed by the weather rather than by time. His black hair had no silver touches, nor had it changed from its porcupine style. It never seemed to grow any longer, nor did it ever appear any shorter.

Quon Lee continued to eat. He gave me the choice of whether to answer or not. I drank some more, hearing the traffic stop at the corner signal light several feet away.

"Loren Balfour's suicide," I said after mentally searching for other possible answers to his question. They all boiled down to that anyway.

"He not make death."

I looked at him as he wiped his mouth with a napkin, then pushed the paper plate aside. It wavered slightly in the breeze.

"You mean he didn't commit suicide?" I set my cup down on the matching saucer. My heart beat faster.

He picked up everything, including my cup, and for a moment I wondered if my question had offended him in some way. I stared off, not moving. But he came back again with it filled to the top of a pink petal. He drank his coffee from a Styrofoam cup.

"I come Sunday. Eight morning. Every Sunday Loren come. Drive down to parking lot." He waved toward the Balfour building next door and the driveway alongside it from Main Street. "Then a lady come. Walk down the alley." He gestured behind his diner to the alley that led off Nutwood, and went into the Balfour parking lot.

"A lady? Who? Where did she come from?" I jolted forward. "Every Sunday?"

"Which question I answer, lawyer?" He smiled.

In spite of the multitude of questions and possible answers in my mind, I had to laugh. His son, Sammy, was an attorney also. But Quon Lee was right; I had asked too many questions at once. Not allowed in the courtroom.

"Who was the lady?"

Quon Lee shook his head slowly. Did that mean he didn't know or he wasn't naming the person?

"What is her name?"

He pointedly stared over my shoulder. Then I turned. The First Methodist Church sat across the street.

I looked back at him. "She came from the church?"

"Too early," Quon Lee said. I could tell he enjoyed this, taking me down one path, then steering me off to another.

"She parked there?"

"Meybee."

I took that to mean he didn't know for sure. "She drove?"

"Not see. Meybee. She wear shoes..." he looked at mine. "Bigger." He stretched his thumb and forefinger.

"She wore a higher heel, not planning on doing a lot of walking in them?"

He smiled and nodded.

"She went into Balfour's?"

He nodded again, drinking from the Styrofoam, but still watching me. As though he sat in the witness box and I had only one chance to ask him the right questions. I wondered why the game, but I had to admit he was right. I knew better. Working in my hometown made me forget my professionalism. I had to learn from the man who gave me candy the first day I toddled to his diner with my mother.

"In spite of the fact Balfour's is closed on Sunday, is that correct?" I gave him a mock serious look.

Quon Lee nodded again. Only his eyes showed how much he enjoyed all of this.

"Someone who worked there?"

Quon Lee shook his head.

"What time did she come?"

"Nine. Always nine."

"Every Sunday?"

Nod.

"How long did she stay?"

"To fifteen before eleven."

I turned again and looked at the church. "Services start at eleven." Quon Lee said nothing. But then I hadn't asked a question. The hot October sun made me feel warm.

"Tell me exactly what she did when she left Balfour's."

"She walk there." He said, pointing to the church.

"Back where she came from?" I said.

Nod.

"Did you see her drive off?"

"Too busy, too many cars."

Yes, the driveway would be filled with cars arriving for the eleven o'clock morning service. And Quon Lee would be busy getting ready for the coffee drinkers and lunch eaters.

I drank from the apple blossoms, the depleting liquid revealing the rest of the branch. I studied its delicate pattern for a moment. So beautiful. Then I said, "An hour and forty-five minutes. Only she and Loren are in the store all that time?" Actually, not a long time.

"I see no other person," he said.

At that moment a man came, waved, and went into the diner. Quon Lee's assistant, I guessed. Sammy used to do that. Close to lunchtime, I only had a few minutes left.

"What did Loren do afterwards?"

Quon Lee had a little smile on his face. "He drive away."

"Why did she come, Quon Lee?"

"Loren have mid-life crisis." He leaned back in the chair and gave a small sigh as though he'd been waiting to say that to someone.

I opened my mouth, not sure of what my next question would be, but Quon Lee said, "You do very good, Jo. I tell Sammy. We play this game. Sammy question me about something. I always tell the truth, but no extra. That's what he say to do."

"Does Sammy know what you've told me?"

"No, he never ask."

"I'm the only one you've told?"

Suddenly the smile dissipated. "I think about this all day, all night. I think and think. That is why I know he did not do death. I think about who to tell. I wait for a sign. Then you come and ask."

"Quon Lee, how do you know that he didn't—"

"If he do death, how he see his Sunday morning lady friend again?"

Chapter 3
Monday 11:30 A.M.

Quon Lee had told me the truth, but nothing extra. Exactly as he said. And certainly not all that he knew. I had to question him again. He didn't tell me the identity of the woman, which I was sure he knew. Some gentlemanly need to protect her? To get that I had to ask the right question. At the right time.

For now I had to be satisfied. Someone else, besides me, didn't believe Loren committed suicide. I didn't know whether I felt better about that or not.

With these thoughts swirling in my mind, I went next door to Balfour's, walking down the alley behind the diner just like the Sunday morning lady friend.

The store's big glass doors opened to the parking lot. Really the front door now in this auto age. Not the door on Main Street that had served that purpose for pedestrians years ago. Once inside, I veered right toward the hallway. At the end, the door to the stockroom, although ajar, was crisscrossed with yellow 'police crime scene' tape. I leaned in.

"Jo."

I jerked back. "Hi, Cal. Just wanted to look around." I could tell he wasn't pleased to see me. Eat dust, Cal. Knowing a lot about him made me wiser, affected how I dealt with him.

He stood at the other end of the room, leaning over the heavy wooden desk. In profile, his stomach sagged over his low belt. He turned back to whatever he'd been reading. The desk, circa 1930, was strewn with papers that looked as if they'd been there just as long. In fact, everything in the room looked like it had been left there for the same period of time.

"What are you doing?" Get him on the defensive.

I ducked under the tape. From where I stood, it looked like he was flipping through the crime report that I hadn't received yet.

"Eric's going to meet me here, do a walk-through."

"Sounds like a play."

"It is. A death play."

"I used to baby sit Eric and Bob when I was going to high school. Hard to believe they're twins. Bob always hibernated in his room with a book while Eric and I watched TV or played board games. Long time ago." Babble on, Jo.

He looked up from the report and held my eyes for a minute. I wondered what he thought, what he remembered, what he wanted me to remember.

"That was twenty years ago."

High school. That's what he was talking about.

Ignoring his comment, I scanned the room. God, what a dismal place. Sagging cardboard boxes piled almost to the ceiling along the wall opposite the door, grey cement floor, worktable top obliterated with old newspapers, manila envelopes, twine, plain wrapping paper and sundry other junk. Just walking in here could make anyone want to commit suicide. Not that I had been too far from it at one point, but I hadn't taken that extra step, the final one. Couldn't. Had Loren?

I looked up at the transom-size window above the desk where Cal stood. Glass and frame had been painted over so that now it became part of the wall. And like the rest of the room, the pale thickened paint caught the dust of years.

The chair was made of sturdy but scarred wood with bronze studs outlining the dark brown, now cracked leather upholstery. Old as the desk. Maybe as old as the building.

"Is it all right if I stand on it?" I nodded toward the chair.

Cal frowned. "We've already dusted it. Some latents. Probably not worth anything."

Then he gave me a look that said I was intruding on his time. Too bad, Cal.

I climbed up and sank into the seat cushion. Hard to keep my balance. About as easy as walking on a water bed gracefully. Bending once and holding onto the back of the chair, I straddled the seat and stood on the padded arms. I wanted to go through the whole act. Make all the movements Loren made. Get into his mind.

16

Were some of his thoughts still hovering there in the air?

At my height, 5'10", I could reach the brass and glass pneumatic tube. Loren was 5'7" the Prelim autopsy report had informed me. I bent my knees a little to lower my height, then pantomimed throwing the cord over it.

Up higher, the pipe above the tube looked sturdier. Why hadn't Loren used that? Too high? Did he try? Maybe he threw the cord up there? The dust and grit looked disturbed. Perhaps he did and failed. Maybe he had to settle for a sure thing, what he could reach, not the pipe but the tube.

There were some clean lines as if the cord had squiggled around a bit on the tube. From testing what weight the cord would hold when he first threw it over?

I thought about what else that meant. Loren dangling at the end, struggling, the rope slithering, jumping with his jerky movements to save himself.

I wavered for a moment, dizzy, then gripped another part of the tube, feeling the grit dig into my fingers. I looked down until the dizziness passed.

I had to do this. I had to know everything.

Starting again, I went through the motions of wrapping the electrical cord around the tube, keeping my knees bent a little. The phantom cord went around my neck as I pantomimed tying the noose securely in front, thinking about where the plug ends would be.

What were you thinking, Loren? Life that bad for you? But what was so bad? Win, your wife? Your three children, now grown? Finances? What did the Main Street Project mean to you?

I wondered whether Loren tied the cord around his neck first and then fastened it to the tube. Or the other way around. How exactly did he tie it? I could look at the cord, probably in the property room at the police department where evidence is kept.

I realized the marks in the dust were almost the length of my arm away. Not directly overhead. I looked down at the chair. Loren couldn't kick the chair over, it was too heavy. He'd been conscious long enough to scratch his throat, trying to pull the cord away, maybe having second thoughts. Why couldn't he get his feet back on the arm of the chair?

Maybe he hadn't been able to. Maybe when he stepped off, the cord had jerked him farther away.

We're all your friends, Loren. We didn't want you to do this, so why did you? Why did you hurt us like this?

My head's exactly in the same spot as yours, Loren, tell me what you were thinking, tell me...

Death.

My thoughts blurred.

Dizzy again.

I grabbed at the tube but couldn't reach it. I swayed.

"Get down from there, Jo. What do you think you're doing?"

"Leave me alone, Cal. I'm just doing my job, same as you." There were blank holes in my vision. I climbed down clumsily.

"That isn't part of your job." He stood up straight now. The police officer on duty.

"I told you that I want to know why a person we knew, a friend of ours, a pillar of the community, for no known reason, hangs himself. I want to know why." I glared at him. Defiant.

Cal's eyes were black as he glared back.

Standoff.

"Hi."

Cal and I abruptly swiveled our heads to the voice.

Eric Balfour.

Thick, black hair falling on his forehead emphasized the paleness of his face. With his short-sleeve, light tan shirt and chino pants, he blended well into the monochromatic room. He gave me a hug. The little boy I had baby sat was old enough now to have his own kids.

I made my escape as soon as I could. About to bend under the tape across the doorway, I glimpsed something red on the packing table. A bow as red as a maraschino cherry surrounded by all that beige. Why hadn't I noticed it before?

It looked like a gift of some sort, but was almost completely covered with detritus as though someone had hastily tried to hide it. I wanted to go over and look at it but Eric was there. Did I want him watching me paw through his father's things?

The red bow was the only color in the stockroom besides the yellow crime scene tape draped on the doorway.

Chapter 4
Monday Afternoon

I ran two flights of stairs from the hospital parking lot, my heart already pounding from the moment Audrey told me that my mother had been taken to Emergency by the paramedics.

"So, Maggie Pie…went and broke your leg, did you?" Doctor Delbert Webster was talking to mother when I ran into the hospital room. I stood for a moment leaning against the doorframe as my heart tried to rocket out of my skin.

"She's okay, clean break," Dr. Del said to me. "Why don't you sit down for a few minutes, or else I'll have to be looking after you, too."

"Hi honey, how are you?" Mother's voice was weak; I almost didn't recognize it. With no makeup and hair uncombed, she looked old. I nodded and waved, trying to smile, too breathless to speak.

I sat heavily, panting, onto the grey plastic and chrome chair, its legs squeaking on the green tile floor, wondering why I had reacted the way I had. Blood is thick. Particularly when it's the same as your mother's.

"Let's see how the traction's holding for now." I watched Dr. Del lift the sheet labeled "always rented never sold" and feel inside the blue leg-long splint. "Good."

"Glad one of us likes it," Mother said.

"Do I detect a little sarcasm there?" Dr. Del said.

"Not just a little."

I wanted to say something between gasps. Anything. Now that I knew Mother wasn't dying, nothing more critical than a broken leg, I could feel the adrenaline ebbing away, anxiety fading, anger rising as though she'd broken her leg on purpose to lure me over to visit her. And I didn't want to think that she actually did that.

19

"Are you having a little discomfort, Maggie?" Dr. Del asked in his professional voice.

"Discomfort? Is that what you call it these days, Del? I'm having outright pain. It hurts like sin."

"Your mother," he said to me, "chased this handsome, rich widower, tripped, and fell."

Ordinarily that joke irritated me. It's been part of mother's repertoire of jokes for a long time. Since dad died. It irritated me because it seemed a tasteless joke, as though she didn't think about dad anymore, only of her next conquest. Plus it always reminded me that my father was dead. But now it seemed all right. Everything was almost normal. Mother and I could get back to our battle stations.

"She'll heal nicely," Dr. Del continued, "and then she'll be able to pick up where she left off. Might even be able to catch him this time, right, Maggie?"

"That's why I broke my leg, so all the handsome, rich bachelors could visit me here. Maybe feel sorry for me."

"I'm not any of those," Dr. Del said. "And if you think that, you need new glasses, too," he said.

They both laughed. I watched my mother's face. Pain etched her lines deeper. Her black hair, limp and tangled, was not her usual coiffure. White showed at the roots. As though she was naked and helpless. Somehow that frightened me.

"Maybe you need new glasses when you see yourself. You look just fine," Mother said.

"I'm not rich either," Dr. Del said. In contrast, his hair, silver and tousled, always looked that way, as though he was too worried and concerned about his patients to take the time to comb it. "I'm thinking more about retiring than I am working harder. I have to keep at it as long as my old friends keep breaking their legs."

"Delbert, don't you dare retire until you fix me up and get me out of here." This time it came out in an angry whisper.

Mother. Maggie Ralston Peters she billed herself. Sounded like a name that should have III after it.

"I promise." He covered her leg with the sheet, checked the five-pound traction again, then tied the edge of the sheet to the bed frame. At that moment a white-garbed nurse came in wheeling a high tray of paper cups and other paraphernalia. Dr. Del nodded to her.

"We'll step out into the hall for a few minutes."

I stood as he came over to me. He put a hand under my elbow and steered me into the hallway.

"She's okay? Really?" I asked when we were outside the room, looking at him for any signs to the contrary.

"Fine. Broken leg, that's all. No complications. She'll be up and around in no time. It will slow her down, but not too much." The lips under his mini-broom moustache widened, showing white, ad-perfect teeth.

I breathed out in relief. I felt everything in my body relax. "How did it happen," I started to ask, then suddenly felt tired. I didn't want to know. What did it matter? Her leg was broken, that was it.

"She could use a good rest. Of course, this isn't what she had in mind. Even on vacation she goes at top speed, trying to see everything, do everything."

I didn't answer. I knew they vacationed together. Did a lot of things together, but did not live under the same roof. Dr. Del's decision, not mother's. If she had her way, and she usually did, some day that would change. What could he tell me about her?

Now that I knew mother was not at death's door, my thoughts were on Dr. Del's other position in the community. "You did the preliminary coroner's report on Loren?" The one I'd held in my hands on Monday.

He stared off down the corridor, silent for a few moments. "I've seen a few suicides in my day, but that doesn't mean I understand why they do it."

"What about Loren? Do you have any idea why he did it?"

Dr. Del shook his head, compressing his lips. We studied each other for a few minutes. He had taken some of the Polaroids.

"Tissue under his fingernails," I said trying to out-noise my other thoughts. That was in the report. "His or someone else's?" That wasn't in the report. There hadn't been enough time for the lab to analyze it, but I asked anyway.

"His, probably. Consistent with the scratches on his throat. Suicides change their minds at the last minute sometimes and try to claw away the noose. It's also an instinctive, human survival reaction. Loren's neck didn't break. Death was caused by strangulation. That's slow and painful, with kicking and struggling. Struggling to get the noose away from the neck or climbing the rope to ease the pressure. This results in scratches and tears of the flesh and ripping loose of fingernails and rope burns on his palms and fingers."

Bile jerked up a few notches to the back of my throat, vividly seeing the colored photos of Loren's body. Thought about the dust disturbed on the pipe. I pushed the image out of my mind.

"What if it's someone else's tissue?"

"I've sent it to the county lab for a report, but I expect them to confirm that it's Loren's. I've kept a couple of samples in case anything gets lost from here to there."

"There's nothing to indicate that it wasn't suicide?"

He looked at me squarely, his eyes searching my face as though trying to read why I had asked the question.

But he didn't answer it.

Chapter 5
Monday 4 P.M.

I left the hospital after checking the time, realizing I'd better go directly to my manicure appointment at 4:00, not back to the office.

Manicure is not the right word, but it's one everyone understands. It's a torture appointment.

My nails are as thin as onion-skin paper, and tear the second they grow even a hair's width. I've done everything but witchcraft, like burying pig's eyes at midnight, and I'd do that if it came with a written guarantee.

The only guarantee is acrylic and gel nails. Voila—instant and durable long nails. I love the way they look. "Real" nails at last.

Acrylic and gel are miracle materials. Dottie pulls off the old, which feels like my whole nail is being lifted off. Dottie is a kind torturer, though. For one hour we chat about movies, people, the world, everything.

Dottie just laughs whenever I try to pull my hand away. She always continues the beautification process, building my nails up to a strong, even length. "Only my mother and you ever complain," she says smiling as though she has paid me a compliment.

I've thought about asking Dottie how much she likes her mother. But I know she does, and it seems a poor joke. Not everyone doesn't get along with her mother.

She covers the nails with new stuff, troweling it on like miniature mortar. The smell of the acrylic is acrid, nose-stunning for someone like me with a great sense of smell. Luckily, it dissipates quickly. It doesn't seem to bother her, for she never wears a mask. After the acrylic, she paints on the gel, then files and buffs. My hands look gorgeous. And I never have to do anything. Except in three weeks present my hands again. It's wonderful. For three weeks.

"You know Loren Balfour committed suicide?" she said.

In a town with no newspaper out yet, she knew. The small town grapevine.

"Yes." Prickles on the back of my neck.

"I saw him Friday night."

"You were at the mixer?" I raced through my memory of the people there. "I didn't see you."

"Picking mom up. Didn't come in. I'm not good at socializing like that. I hate it. Mom loves it." She shrugged, but again she spoke with pride of her mother.

"What happened?"

"I pulled into the parking lot, and as I turned the car around, the headlights were right on him," she said.

"Loren?"

"Yeah, he had that funny plaid jacket on he wears a lot. You know the one I mean, like the kind plaid golfing pants are made of?"

Yes, I knew the jacket well. Loren's trademark. Maybe he had several of them, for his jackets always looked clean and pressed.

"I mean, he didn't look like he was thinking about hanging himself. No way," Dottie said, shaking her head. She gave out a lady-like guffaw. Her long, blonde hair perfectly coiled into one large, smooth ringlet over her left shoulder. The ringlet moved sinuously as she talked. "He was with a woman."

It took me a moment to take in what she said. "Win? His wife?" I felt my eyes widening, mentally processing the meaning of her words.

"Nope. He had his back to me and the woman was standing in front of him. Too short for Win. All's I could see of her was part of her skirt, like polka dots or something."

"No idea who she was?" I said.

"Not a clue," she said. "Didn't exactly hang around to find out."

"I don't remember anyone at the party with polka dots on." Packed with folks. Oktoberfest. I remembered the heat and the crowd in the room and searched my memory for someone wearing polka dots.

"Like I said, he sure didn't look like he was going to go commit suicide. If anything, it seemed like the opposite."

"What do you mean, 'the opposite'?" I said.

"What do I mean? What's the opposite? I mean he was saying hello to life not goodbye."

"Goodbye?"

"Yeah, where are you at today, Jo? Smooching. Big, fat, mushy kisses. They were hugging and kissing like mad. Can't see someone about to commit suicide doing that. I don't even think they knew my headlights were on them. They were that into it."

"Loren kissing a woman in the parking lot at the mixer?"

"Yep. Kind of surprised me. Him being married for such a long time and being a pillar of the community and all that."

"Maybe he was just saying goodnight to a friend?"

Dottie looked up with a sardonic expression on her face. "Yeah, a really good friend."

"You can't describe her other than she wore a polka dot skirt and was shorter than Win?"

"Something like polka dots."

"You're sure it was Loren? Not someone else wearing a jacket like his?"

Dottie shrugged. "I saw what I saw. That's all I know. You never can tell about men. I wouldn't have thought of him as a cheater." She shook her head again.

We were silent for a moment. I tried to visualize Loren smooching in the parking lot. Or any place.

"And then, two days later he commits suicide," said Dottie. "Makes you wonder, doesn't it?"

Chapter 6
Monday 5:00 P.M.

While my nails were drying in little white boxes, each awhirl with a fan, I watched the digital clock slowly changing from one number to the next. I had to sit there and dry them for eight minutes, then be careful afterwards because they really wouldn't set for an hour. I peeked at them as though that would hurry the hardening. I had picked a red polish. That's the kind of kick-ass mood I was in.

Maraschino red!

The package with the bow at Balfour's. The red bow in the beige room. The thought clanged in my head.

Five p.m. I grabbed my car keys and left, hoping Balfour's was still open. Dottie opened her mouth, maybe to tell me my eight minutes weren't up, but I just waved and fled.

The stockroom door was no longer decorated with yellow tape.

And there wasn't anything red on the packing table. The room had returned to its drab tan color. Depression settled over me as though it was part of the decor of the room.

"Hi, Jo." I jumped and whirled around, expecting a ghost.

Ed. He had worked in the store as long as I could remember, but I knew him mostly as an active member of the chamber, and usually one of the bartenders at the mixers.

"Hi. Do you remember something there?" I gestured toward the mess on the counter. "A package with a red bow?"

Ed nodded.

Bingo.

"Police carted it off. Yeah, Cal took it. Real careful putting it in another box. Used a pen through the bow and lifted it up. Like he didn't want to touch it. I kidded him about it exploding, but you know him when he's working, real serious about the whole thing. What was in it? A bomb?" Ed laughed.

"I don't know. I forgot to ask Cal about it when I was here with him." Truth is an elastic band.

Ed seemed eager to tell me more. "Yeah, box with a big red bow." He laughed again. His toupee slipped as usual. "Looked like something from the Jayne's Gift Shoppe, kind of paper they wrap things in. We asked around but nobody fessed up to owning it. You'll have to talk to Cal about it."

"I'll do that. I'm going back to the office now. Wanted to be sure he got it. Thanks, Ed." I started to walk past him down the hallway. I wanted out of the room. But I wasn't going to make it.

"You knew about Sheila, didn't you? Loren's sister?" Ed leaned against the doorway, adjusting his black, synthetic hair. He was half a foot shorter than me, thin, wearing a shiny dark tie, white short-sleeve shirt and navy pants. No more a symphony of color than the room.

"No, what about her?" More prickles on the back of my neck. The room had that aura. I stepped forward. Ed didn't move. I was going to have to hear this story. And I was going to have to stay planted.

"Twenty years ago. Tried to commit suicide in this very room. Same darn tube, too." As though the latter made the act more reprehensible. He pointed past my shoulder, but I didn't turn and look up at the tube. I felt cold all of a sudden. But I was now very interested in his story.

"And she did the same thing. Extension cord. A new one, too."

"You said she tried. She didn't succeed?"

"Almost. Kirby Hawkins was here to pick up Eric. Couldn't find him anywhere so he looked in here. This was off limits to Eric. Nobody wanted him playing in here." He eyed the stacked boxes. "Kirby cut her down right away. Almost unconscious."

"Unconscious? Any brain damage?"

"Not any worse than before," Ed said. "Afterwards they put her up in Milford. She died last year, as a matter of fact."

"Did she...?"

"Nah, natural causes."

Saved from suicide only to be put in an insane asylum. Not

what I'd call a lucky person. Which was the better fate?

Then the thought struck me. Did Loren think he was going insane? Is that why he did it? Not wanting to end up like his sister? But I had detected no strain of insanity in him ever. Someone who tells jokes well can't be too crazy.

Ed's eyes roved around the colorless room. "Since then no one's been too fussy about coming in here. Probably twenty years ago. It sure is a mess." He said that as though he was seeing the room for the first time.

I realized he hadn't stepped in, just stood there leaning against the door frame. No part of his body had crossed the threshold.

"You were here the first time it happened? With Sheila?"

"I was working here. But it was on my day off so I missed all the excitement. Got to hear about it, though."

I thought about Eric. What if he had been in this room? That means he had seen his aunt and now his father commit suicide. Was that possible?

"Where was Eric?"

"Found him later in the men's room, sick as a dog. By then we were closing up the store. Six p.m. He didn't get to go wherever Kirby was taking him off to."

"Maybe that's why they couldn't find him. He was sick," I said.

"Maybe." Ed sounded doubtful.

I knew the Hawkins and the Balfours were old and close friends. Eric was probably going to play with the Hawkins girl. They were about the same age twenty years ago. Another tragedy for our small town when she had died young.

"Thanks, Ed. I'll let you get back to work." He certainly didn't look in any hurry to do any such thing, but then again, there probably weren't any customers to worry about. No work to do. Maybe he just counted the sofas.

I had to get out of the room. No breathable air. "Got to go, Ed, see you at the next chamber meeting. Bye." This time I pushed past him. I brushed against his arm and smelled the faint aroma of aftershave and ancient history.

Chapter 7
Monday 5:30 P.M.

There was a good chance Cal would still be in his office. What were the innards of that package? Thoughts tumbled over each other in my mind like clothes in a dryer. I should give him the information I had from Quon Lee, Dottie and Dr. Del. How much had Ed told him? I wanted to talk, bounce ideas around, although they'd probably only be mine.

Cal's office door had glass in the upper half. I watched him as he stood at his desk, sipping coffee.

I pushed open the door, gave him a moment to adjust to the fact that I was in his face again, and said, "I have some information, and I know you do, too. We'll trade. Then I have to report it all to Deb."

"You mean to that woman from Beverly Hills who comes in here acting like we ought to be grateful she came all the way out here to the boonies to deal with us Neanderthals?" he said.

"That sounds like Deb." I knew she had an abrasive manner about her. Perhaps men found it even more so. To me, she was just being Deb. She was still handling the account, which made her my boss.

Cal waved his cup at the chair in front of his desk. "Coffee?" Cal never had an empty cup. I wondered if the coffee pot ever cooled down long enough for anyone to wash it.

"No." I sat down, took a deep breath, and launched straight into what my two witnesses and what Dr. Del had said.

For a minute he seemed almost interested in the idea of Loren kissing someone in the parking lot, but he waved that off, old as yesterday's news. About the Sunday morning lady friend his comment was, "Probably the bookkeeper or a secretary coming in to catch up on work."

"Quon Lee said she wasn't anyone who worked there."

"How does he know? Could be a part-timer who only comes in on Sunday morning."

"All dressed up and wearing high heels?"

"Could be going to church afterwards. Left her car in the church lot while did a couple of hours of work. Or she could be someone who's already been to Church. Don't you Catholics have an early Mass?" Cal trying to be funny made me suspicious. Like he was performing a sleight of hand trick. Maybe trying to divert my attention to something else. But what? And why?

"I think the woman was Loren's girlfriend," I said.

Cal shrugged, took a sip of coffee, and fiddled with the papers on his desk.

"Tell me about the package you picked up at Balfour's," I said.

He sighed. Probably because he knew he had to give me information which he strew about like Hope diamonds. He studied me for a moment but my jaw was set. "Come on down to property and I'll show you."

When we got to the giant cage known as the property room, Cal unlocked the wire mesh door. The familiar wrapping paper covered with dusting powder rested on one of the deep mental shelves.

"Any prints?"

He nodded.

"Good ones?"

He nodded again.

"Okay, Cal, whose?"

"Loren's. And somebody else's. Depending on whether Loren was giving the gift or getting the gift."

"Getting the gift? Somebody gave it to him in that stockroom? That place has the grime of the Middle Ages. Why was he in there, anyway? No one ever uses it."

Of course, Cal ignored my questions and went on. "We've checked at Jayne's Gift Shoppe, and we're going on the theory the other prints are from the person who wrapped it."

"Haven't you—?"

Cal held up his hand. "Lot of part timers. They've got employees on vacation, honeymoon, maternity leave."

"He was giving the gift, not receiving it," I said, musing out loud. "I think he put it in the stockroom because he didn't want anyone to find it. It looked like someone was trying to hide it with that paper and stuff over it. If he left it in his office, someone might see it and ask questions. Same thing at home." As I talked, my brain censor went on vacation. I saw the hanging expression on Cal's face. You had to know him to catch the slight flicker in his eyes and jaw. I felt as though I'd hit a nerve.

"If he received it, why didn't he open it?" I went on. "There would have been a third set of prints—that of the person who gave it to him."

Cal looked at me for a moment, then responded by pulling the package off the metal shelf and setting it on the counter. He took the top off. Nestled in the tissue paper sat a china figurine, a tableau of a boy and girl beside a palm tree, he in a sarong, strumming on a ukulele, and she in a grass skirt and lei, arms over her head, body curved in a hula movement. The colors were muted and the expressions on their faces intimated they only had eyes for each other. "How lovely," I said, momentarily forgetting why I was looking at it.

A gift for the Sunday morning lady friend.

What did it mean?

I looked at Cal. "You knew about the woman."

Neither of us mentioned Win.

"Worked it out that there had to be one after I saw this."

"Who?"

Cal gave a small shake of his head. "Don't know."

I looked at him hard.

"I mean, I really don't know," he said.

"The woman in the polka dot skirt and the Sunday morning lady friend are one and the same?" I didn't add that I was sure Quon Lee knew who she was. I had to get back to him, hoping his honor as a gentleman could be overcome by the right questions.

"Maybe, maybe not."

I looked at the figurines.

"The woman in the polka dot skirt." I thought about that Friday evening again, and a white light went off in my memory. A flashbulb.

"THE PICTURES," I shouted. "The chamber took pictures that

night. At the mixer. Let's get them." I looked at my watch. Maybe I wouldn't need Quon Lee's information after all, just his verification.

Cal reached for the wall phone. "I'll call Ron and ask him." Ron Deveraux, the chamber director.

After a few moments of pauses and yeses, Cal hung up.

"Come on." He started for the stairs, making sure the mesh door locked shut. "No one's picked them up. Ron forgot all about them so he's calling over to make sure someone will wait for us."

George, the owner of the camera store, met us outside with three orange envelopes. "First time anybody's been hot to get these," he said. "What's so important, Loren?" Not too many secrets in this town.

"Mayor's husband thinks his fly was open," Cal said.

"Oh, right," George said, realizing Cal wasn't going to tell him the real reason. He waved goodnight and went back into his store, locking the door after him. Past closing time.

We sat in the car and went through each of the fat envelopes. No women with a polka dot anything. Not even a polka dot tie.

"She wasn't at the mixer. She must have met him in the parking lot," I said. "Maybe arranged to meet him there."

"She could be shy, not want her picture taken."

"Certainly not kissing Loren," I said. Suddenly I felt tired, drained. I just wanted to go home, put my feet up and have a tall glass of something cold and strong. Preferably someone to make it for me, then massage my neck while I sipped. But those days were gone.

I flipped through the pictures again. Something about the polka dots ghosted in my memory. Dottie had said it was something like polka dots. What else was like polka dots?

"Drop the possible murder idea, Jo." Cal always cut to the quick.

"We've got evidence of a woman—"

"Gossip."

"From two different sources like Dottie and Quon Lee? You can't dismiss the evidence that way, Cal."

"What other points do you want to make, Counselor?" He

started to drive to City Hall.

"No note. He didn't leave a suicide note," I said.

"Doesn't mean anything. Half the time there isn't a note. Great if we had one, wrap it up nice and neat and convince you, the only person in the world who doesn't believe that Loren committed suicide."

I was about to say Quon Lee didn't believe it either, but Cal would probably dismiss that, too.

Cal could sure make me lose my confidence in a hurry. "There's the tissue—"

"There's the tissue," he mimicked me. "If it's Loren's skin that doesn't tell us anything because he had scratches on his neck consistent with suicide. If we get another report that says it's somebody else's skin, then maybe that would mean something. But that's not going to be in the report because the tissue was Loren's. You've got diddly squat in the way of evidence. When the coroner's report comes back, I'm closing the file. It's almost closed already."

We were at City Hall now. "Wait a minute. Both you and Ed said a new electrical cord. What about the packaging? The cardboard band or whatever else was around it. Look for that? Fingerprints on it, maybe? Was it in the stockroom?"

"Didn't find anything in that room. He could have dropped it in the trash in the lamp department or anywhere on his way to the stockroom. He could have opened it a week before. Months before. He could have been planning it for a long time. And, yeah, we did look for it. Know how many trash containers, wastepaper baskets, cardboard boxes and sundry other things in that building that people throw things into?"

"Never mind." I opened the door. Why was I arguing with him? Masochism.

"You don't understand the politics of this," he said. "The chief wants a nice quiet suicide. The city manager wants a nice quiet suicide. I want a nice quiet suicide. Makes the town seem safer than a murderer running around loose."

"That's no reason to say it was a suicide." My voice was rising. I was going to be yelling in a minute. Cal could do that to me. "What about the politics of the wrongful death suit if it was suicide? Would you rather have that?"

He leaned across the seat. "Not 'if.' It was suicide. You haven't said anything about this to anyone else have you?"

I shook my head. "No." Why was he asking me that?

"Forget what I just said. The case is closed. I want you to stay in that conference room office of yours and do nothing but read all the reports I send you. Just deal with the wrongful death suit if there is one. I don't want you to investigate so much as a parking ticket if Loren happened to have one."

"Don't tell me what to do," I shouted at him. I knew I was sounding childish. Cal sure knew how to bring out the best in me.

"I'm ordering you. Don't run around town talking about murder to anyone. You hear me?"

"You're ordering me! I'm not one of your minions who has to jump to your bidding because of some secret police code."

"Stay in your office." He waved a finger just like our old physics teacher.

"You look like cranky, Mr. Whitby." I slammed the door as hard as I could. Cal roared off, tires squealing and engine revving like he was on a NASCAR race track.

I felt like jumping up and down and screaming at him. Instead, I fumed as I watched his car disappear down the street. I took a few deep breaths. What was it worth to me to have a tantrum fit, which I jolly well felt like doing? I had to calm myself down. I think Cal liked to get a rise or a reaction out of people. Me in particular, I was sure. Why? Because it made him feel more in control? I'd have to ask my psychiatrist friend about that.

My brain clicked in. How come he knew about all the trash containers at Balfour's?

He had searched them.

Why did he do that if it was such a cut-and-dried case that Loren had committed suicide? He said it was similar to other suicides, so it must be one.

Was it prestidigitation again? Diverting my attention away from the fact that he'd revealed something to me when he told me about his search for the cord? Not meaning to. Was that why he tried to get my ire up? And did.

I smiled. Gotcha, Cal!

I called Deb, left a message on her voice mail telling her about the suicide, its possible wrongful death action, and told her I'd send a report.

I dictated a memo briefly summarizing the facts, the ones in the prelim and the crime report. Everything all nice and legal-like. No suppositions or guesses or gut feelings even hinted at.

My thoughts switched to a darker track, surprised that I hadn't been dwelling on it before. I'd been too busy trying to convince Cal it wasn't a suicide. Now I realized why he wanted it to be one, and why he told me to back off.

If Loren didn't kill himself, someone else did.

Maybe someone in this town did it.

Maybe someone I knew.

A murderer in our midst?

Chapter 8
Monday to Tuesday

That night I had a dream about the girl in the red dress, a dream I hadn't had for years. A relief from my other dream, in a way. Is it a dream when it was something that really happened?

I was a freshman, and he was a senior, captain of the football team and darn good at it. With those smiling blue eyes of his, he had all the girls in love with him.

One morning at school, he walked toward me in the hall. I didn't know whether to smile at him or not. I knew who he was, but I didn't think he knew me. Seniors didn't acknowledge freshmen.

He kept walking toward me. "Hey," he said, "I tried to call you last night, but your line was busy." My heart stopped. The whole world stopped. He tried to call me? He dialed my number? He knew who I was?

I tried to remember why the telephone had been busy so that I could explain. But instead what came out was the question, "Why were you calling?" As though my mind and mouth weren't in sync.

"There's a basketball game on Saturday and I thought you might like to go with me. A friend gave me some tickets." His eyes sent warm messages. My heart pounded faster. "You were probably talking to one of your boyfriends," he said.

I started to say I had no boyfriends, but ended up just saying yes to Saturday night. How eager I was. How excited.

The basketball game and then many dates after that. I was the envy of many.

Until the dance.

A big dance. Two other high schools in the area came. Chaperoned, yes, but most of the boys had flasks and bottles hidden in the bathroom, cars, lockers, everywhere. So when he toddled off saying "see you in a bit," I thought I knew where he was going.

I stayed in the gym listening to the music and watching the couples dance for a while, but it was hot and no one else asked me to dance, knowing who I had come with. I wandered down the hall. It was cooler and I wanted to get away.

There, in an alcove, I saw him kissing a girl in a red dress. I watched them for a moment not wanting to believe it. Stunned. Immobile. Staring.

Then I ran back to the dance.

By the time he returned he was quite drunk. Still cute and cuddly as a panda bear. But too drunk to dance, tripping, stumbling, as though his feet were the size of tennis rackets. Out of it.

Still in that state, he was laughing, smiling, pleasant, loveable. A jolly drunk.

One voice in my mind kept saying he was too drunk to know what he was doing when he kissed the girl in the red dress. But the other voice said, he will always be that way, he will always be kissing girls in red dresses. Which voice should I listen to? My heart said the former, my head said the latter.

I wanted that picture of him as a sloppy drunk engraved in my mind. It made it easier. I held on to that mind engraving for a long time. For as long as it took. And it took a long time.

He came over the next afternoon, not outwardly affected by all that alcohol, but I had a hammer-pounding headache from little sleep and a lot of crying. I knew what I had to do.

I went out to the car with him. As he started to turn the ignition key, I said, "I want to talk to you." My heart pumped so hard that it made me dizzy.

"Okay." Smiling blue eyes. He turned to me, leaned back against his window, put his arm on the back of the seat, and wiggled a finger on my shoulder. The picture of nonchalance. I couldn't look at his eyes, his smile because I knew if I did I wouldn't be able to go through with it.

I probably gulped a few times, the freshman vs. the senior. I remember my throat being dry. "I saw you last night kissing that girl."

His finger stopped.

"Yeah? So?"

I don't know what I expected him to say, maybe apologize, deny it, say something. "I thought you were trying to tell me something, like you're moving on to your next girlfriend." I choked the words out.

"No," he said. "I'm not ready to move on. And I won't be for a long time."

He was making it hard for me. I wanted to believe him. I glanced at him. His eyes weren't smiling anymore. He took his arm off the back of the seat. "So what's the problem?"

"Do you remember kissing her?"

"Yeah, sort of."

I wanted to dissect the scene by asking him questions. Who kissed whom, did you enjoy it, does she kiss better than me, on and on ad nauseam. "I don't like that," I said, staring through the windshield which I examined in minute detail. I wanted to look at him, see that familiar face, those blue eyes that made me feel lightheaded with love.

"I don't like how you are when you drink. You're a different person. I like you when you don't drink. I like you a lot." I think I babbled some other things into the windshield. I struggled to keep from crying. Maybe I didn't have any more tears left. My heart beat fast. I felt sick. I could hardly get the words out of my dry throat.

"I can't promise you I won't ever kiss another girl, and I can't promise you I won't have another drink," he said.

"I guess that's it then."

"Okay, now can we go to the movies?" He reached for the ignition, but there must have been something in my face—clenched jaw, cold eyes—because he stopped in mid-movement.

"I mean," I said, gulping a few times, "that's it."

"I don't understand." He was truly puzzled.

So I got out of the car, and walked away. Away, away. He sat there for quite a while. I could see him from my upstairs bedroom.

Then Cal drove off.

Cal left me alone for a while afterwards, not exactly ignoring me, but everyone knew. Of course for a while everyone thought Cal just got tired of me as he had all the others. It meant I joined an elite, but large, group of old girlfriends who eyed his current one with malice as they had me, mixed with the knowledge that she'd be joining them soon. They never eyed Cal with malice. Who could hate him?

I went along with it, didn't say anything, not even to my best friend. It hurt too much to talk about him.

Then the word got out that he wasn't the one to end the dating. He wasn't taking anyone else out. Something was different. Maybe he said something while he was drunk. Or everyone noticed the absence of a new girlfriend. Maybe it was the latter or maybe it was some other reason, he started to pursue me with a vengeance. Not much at school, but he'd be waiting for me at the bus stop near home when I got off, or he'd show up at some place where he knew I'd be, or call me and ask me for a date.

I remember one Saturday night he phoned. He was across the street at a friend's house and asked me to come over. I wanted to so much. So much.

I said no, biting the inside of my mouth and digging my nails into my palms to remind myself of the pain I had felt and still felt. After all it was just across the street, he said, and I could go home any time I wanted. I was afraid if we talked some more, and if I listened to his voice, I would walk across the street.

I told him I was going someplace else. There was silence on the line, and eventually we both hung up.

After that we were just friends. It's a small town, and our paths crossed often that year. Sometimes I thought I saw a look of amusement on his face as though we were sharing a secret joke. But who knew what Cal thought?

Then he went away to the Marines, and I went to Cal State L.A. When he came back and started there as a freshman, I was a senior. And I didn't date freshmen. Every time I saw him, the old hurt came back.

I wondered how Rachel stood all the other girls. Rachel Streeter who came to town and married Cal. Everyone wondered why Rachel, of all people, when Cal had his pick of all the girls, many more attractive than Rachel.

They met when she worked as a nurse at Mirasol General in the Emergency Room and Cal was a sergeant on the Mirasol Police Department. Maybe he felt it was about time to get married.

I never understood their relationship, especially since I knew Cal still kissed girls in red dresses.

Maybe Rachel didn't care. Maybe that's what made their marriage a good one. Maybe that's why Rachel stayed with him. Maybe the nurse in her took care of the drunk in him. The hole in her head fits the protrusion in his, as psychiatrists try to define the symbiosis in odd relationships.

Tuesday morning when I woke up, I related the dream about him to my having a problem. I had to do something, make a decision, as I had all those years ago. Should I keep on trying to find evidence to convince Cal or drop it? Walk away.

If I wasn't fully committed to getting the evidence, then I'd better give it up.

So I made a decision

I'd see this to the end. I'd get the evidence that Loren hadn't committed suicide.

Because I knew there had to be some.

Chapter 9
Tuesday 9:30 A.M.

I decided to do something I hadn't been able to do when I worked at the D.A.'s office or at the law firm in Century City—attend the announcement of the Grand Marshal for the Tournament of Roses Parade in nearby Pasadena.

I could have justified it on the Mirasol clock since we had a float in the parade, but I went on my own time. Deb had told me not to bill more than twenty hours a week and I was easily over that number.

The short ceremony was held every year on the lawn of the Tournament House, a white colonial mansion built on many acres in the early 1900s when land and labor were low in cost and the wealth of the magnate from the east high.

Every group entering a float in the New Year's Day parade was invited to be the first to learn the name of the Grand Marshall— kept a secret until that moment.

Opposite the steps of the spacious side veranda where the secret would be divulged were jean and T-shirted men and women of the media, heavy with the paraphernalia of their profession, getting ready for the event. In contrast, dark-suited tournament members stood casually talking on the pathways of the adjoining rose garden.

I turned as Kirby Hawkins, a long-time clothing store owner in Mirasol, sat down beside me on a white, wooden folding chair. It sank into the grass under his six-foot-tall frame covered with a few more pounds than needed. At the same moment, a man came out and said, "Our Grand Marshall is lost, but will be here in a few minutes." I looked at my Mickey Mouse watch. Still early. I glanced at the speaker. He smiled as though he had just told a joke.

"Somebody who's a geographer," a person behind us said.

"A navigation expert," came from another voice as people tried to guess who the famous person might be from the hint just given. I deduced that hints like that were part of the annual program.

"They should have you guide them," I said to Kirby.

On a Mirasol group trip five years ago to visit our sister city in China, one of my rare vacations while I was at the D.A.'s office, we had stopped over in London for a few days. We were several levels down in the Underground trying to figure out which way to go. Kirby knew right away which direction was north. How he could determine that fact so far down amazed me. He hadn't even looked at the map on the wall. He had a built-in compass.

"Lots of guessing goes on just before the announcement," Kirby said, as we heard other people throwing out names and occupations.

"It's so thrilling for me to be able to attend at last. I'm sure it's all old hat to you after all these years," I said, for I was sure he attended every year.

"It's funny you should say that. I remember Sheila, that's Loren's sister, saying exactly that same thing the first time she came here, years ago. Did you know..." He acted as raconteur, his favorite occupation, about the individuals of Mirasol, where he'd been born and lived all of his sixty-plus years. He sprinkled in asides like a true storyteller and had me laughing, his humor always contagious.

When he paused for a breath, I said, "I was planning to stop by to see you. Since you brought her up, I wanted to ask you some questions about her Sheila trying to commit suicide."

"Just last year we went up for her funeral, took Eric with us. Died of congestive heart failure. Very nice ceremony, even though it wasn't in the family church." I wondered if he meant that as a recommendation for the Mitford facility's administration or as a negative comment about Loren as her guardian.

I moved on with my questions. "You're the one who saved her life." Flattery usually worked. "I want to know more about how she tried to kill herself."

"Loren's suicide brought it all back to me. Remembered that day like it was yesterday. Terrible thing, just terrible. Sheila was never the stable one, but Loren was. My friend. You just can't tell about people." He bowed his head as though trying to control his emotions about his old friend.

"Did he copy her? Ed said that you were there, and that she'd used a new electrical cord, too. How similar was the method?" Of what importance was that? I was asking too many questions at the same time, but I hoped to trigger his memory. Maybe all I was doing was upsetting him.

Kirby stared off into the space of the green lawn and trees, probably not seeing any of it, only what was on his mind's screen. "Can't say that I paid too much attention to the details when I got Sheila down. Just like you said, a new electrical cord. Guess Loren did the same thing, but I don't know that for a fact. You would." He turned to me as he spoke. I didn't give him any response, waiting for him to continue.

"That's all I remember. I noticed because the knots weren't tight. Understand Eric had to use a knife."

Since he hadn't asked a question, I didn't respond to that either, thinking of the game Quon Lee had played with me. Also, I didn't know how much of the information about Loren's death was still under wraps. Instead, I asked another question. "She used that old chair?"

"That old brown thing? It's still there? Yes, that's what she used."

"So sad," I said. "I just can't believe Loren did it."

"Must run in the family. Funny she didn't try it long before, when her father broke up her romance with Charlie Quinn. No reason to do that except he was at odds with Charlie's father—they had stores practically next door on Main Street. Some argument they got into. Never really clear on what it was."

"Why didn't they run away, elope?"

"Not in those days. Family ties too strong. Just wasn't done. Today, yes, but not then. Different kind of world then. Town different, too, and—"

A trumpet blare signaled the imminent announcement and effectively silenced Kirby, as not many things did.

But it didn't silence my thoughts.

Chapter 10
Tuesday Morning Later

"Okay, Maggie Pie, try that again," Dr. Del said as I stepped into the hospital room.

"You just treat us like we're your dolls," mother said. "You dress us up, put pins in us, make us move this and that." Her voice sounded a little irritated. I'd heard that often enough.

"You are my doll," he said to her. "So move that leg. Good. Again. Good. No discomfort, right?" Dr. Del moved professional fingers over her leg and foot.

"You mean 'no pain,' you old buzzard. No, it feels wonderful. How do you think a leg that's been broken every which way feels?" Her voice still held impatience and annoyance, but she reined it in.

"I can remember back in the old days—" Dr. Del said.

"You might, but I can't. You're a lot older than I am," mother said.

"Dream on, Maggie. Must be that hallucinogen I'm giving you."

"You need to take some yourself." They both laughed, mother first. Maybe she thought she had gone too far.

"Your mother's feeling better," Dr. Del said.

No kidding. I produced a smile and a nod.

"Just rest a bit, Maggie. I'll be right back," he said.

I gave mother a little wave, communicating the same thing.

I walked out and heard them laugh again. In a few minutes Dr. Del came out.

Thoughts and emotions swirled. I didn't like being in a hospital. The shining floors did not give off the aroma of being freshly waxed. It was the aroma of pain and depression and confinement. But maybe that was the mood I was in, feeling all three of those things.

"Did you bring the sample?" I said, trying to sound casual. Audrey had called him with the request.

He had a bulky brown envelope, but held onto it. He looked at me. "Why are you all of a sudden all fired up to get a tissue report from a private pathology lab? No question they're going to be faster than the county." He waited for an answer. And he looked like he wasn't going to give me the envelope until I told him.

"It's important to do all the paperwork in case Win files suit for a wrongful death." I know I looked down at the envelope like it was a fix. Maybe it was. A fix for my life, finding out for sure whether or not Loren committed suicide. Whether I should be guilty of sins of omission. There wasn't anything I could have done for Nate, my law partner, as many times as I had thought of that day. Guilt about Nate had turned into guilt about Loren? Because I couldn't stop the killing of either of them?

Dr. Del nodded. Paperwork he understood. Maybe he also understood about not asking too many questions and not finding out something he didn't want to know. He handed over the envelope. Maybe he just wanted to be sure he wasn't doing something illegal.

"How's mother doing?" I said, changing the subject.

"Fine. As I've said before, she's going to mend fast and be as energetic as ever."

"Good."

"Now if you want to know how she's doing emotionally, I can't answer that."

"What do you mean?" Now I had asked a question I didn't want to know the answer to.

"It's none of my business, Jo, but I've known you both for a long time. If I wanted to be cute about this, I could say that I prescribe you spend a little more time with her."

I turned away, looking out of the window at the end of the hall. Wanting to walk through it, over the trees and up the green hill away from a wound.

"She's really a nice person, but I'm sure you know that," Dr. Del said.

I turned back to him. "Thanks for everything." I gave him a

quick kiss on the cheek.

He seemed a little embarrassed and glanced at his watch. "I'd better get moving and see Marti."

It took a moment before the name registered. "Marti? You mean Kirby's wife?"

Dr. Del nodded, already mentally on his rounds.

"What's she in for?" As if it was a prison term.

"Looks like a bad case of the flu. Can't find anything else wrong with her. She was dehydrated, weak, but she's healthy otherwise. Getting back some tests so I'll be able to tell a little more."

"She's not—"

Dr. Del turned, and looked at me. "She'll be okay, Jo, just like your mother is going to be okay." He looked like he was about to say something else, but didn't.

I watched him hurry down the hall.

Where was it written you have to like your mother?

I went back to my office at City Hall, gave the tissue sample to Audrey to send out for a report, private and rush rush rush. It would be expensive, but it would also answer my major question. She looked as if she wanted to make a comment, but didn't.

I had seen Skip Louis, Head of the Planning Department, sitting in his office, writing. He was visible through the window that faced the parking lot. His office handled the Main Street Project. I thought I'd pay him a visit.

"Hi, have time for a couple of questions?" It didn't matter what he said because I was in and sitting down before he answered.

"Sure, but the only time I get a visit from the city attorney's office is when there's some humongous lawsuit going on with my name right there at the top, and they're going to take my first born."

I laughed. Too close to the truth to be really funny. Then again, I wondered if he brought problems on himself by not being diplomatic when he was taking people's property from them by the condemnation process.

"And how is your baby?" Safe territory, get him off the offense. Skip handed me two framed pictures. "She doesn't have a moustache," I said looking at Skip's toothbrush-size one.

He nodded, but whether there was a smile on his face, I couldn't tell. I sensed the amenities were over. I looked at his long-sleeve, subtly-striped white shirt. He would look just as fresh at the end of the day, while I would be crumpled and soaked.

He sat back in his chair, forming a tent with his fingers. Waiting.

"I want to know about the Main Street Project."

"Ah ha, so we are being hit with a suit? I knew it."

"Nothing's surfaced yet. I just want to be put in the picture. What's the plan? How did the Balfour store fit into it? That sort of thing." Too many questions, but he could take his pick.

"In twenty words or less?"

I laughed again, acknowledging his humor.

"The plan is basically simple." He sounded as if he had given the speech many times. "Tear down the entire block of commercial buildings on the north side of Main from Nutwood to Durban. As you know, only some of the businesses are still operating, but the rest have been closed for years."

"Balfour's, Quon Lee's, and what?"

"The old department store next to Balfour's. In actuality, it's not operating as the original business, but the owners are leasing booths to individuals and having art and craft shows on the weekends. In fact, the concept is working so well we're thinking of incorporating the idea into the new project. People love it."

"Translated means it's making money, and generating votes."

Skip smiled. At least he stretched his lips. The tented fingers were moving back and forth like a spider doing slow pushups on a mirror.

"How does Balfour's fit into this?" I said.

"Going to be torn down for the site of the anchor store. We wanted to start there first. Start generating some tax money. Get the downtown economy jump started."

"'Going to be?' As in future tense?"

"Loren stopped the project. He got a court order." The left corner of his mouth lifted slightly and his tone sounded bitter. "That threw all the plans off."

"A stay? But that only halts it for ninety days. So what does that mean?" I said.

"It means, Jo, that Loren Balfour made a lot of people mad. The city council for one, because every day the project doesn't go forward, the city's losing sales tax dollars. Which means we can't make any revenue projections. Which affects our bond status, dropping us from quadruple A. Which means that we have less of a chance of selling bonds to raise capital for the project."

Skip hit the desk with the side of his right hand on the downbeat of each "which."

"It also means every day we delay the building costs go up. And that makes a lot of people mad." One of those people appeared to me to be Skip.

"The biggie is that we could lose the federal funding for the project if we don't start it by a certain date."

I nodded, but he continued without my encouragement.

"All the other owners on that block were mad at him because he ruined the only chance they've had for years, not only to sell their property, but to get a good price for it. Eric and Bob were mad at him because they wanted to sell, get a new store. Quon Lee was mad at him because Loren's resistance meant his site wouldn't be part of any project, so he sued Loren—"

"Quon Lee sued Loren?" Why hadn't he mentioned that? I hadn't played the game, asked the right questions.

"I guess it was the last straw for Quon Lee. Said he's put up with Loren all these years. The driveway easement and the parking lot which they were supposed to share. Quon Lee gave Loren supposedly half of the costs of repaving. Loren took the money but didn't do anything. I'm sure he's not sorry Loren went to the big store in the sky."

Quon Lee had sued Loren? All of the things he had told me-- were they the truth? Because that's the path I was on. Was there really a Sunday morning lady friend or had he said that just to throw me off the scent? Divert my attention as Cal had tried to do? Was that why Cal took the idea of a woman who went there on Sunday morning with a grain of salt? Because he knew Quon Lee made up the story for some reason?

We sat there for a moment, each with our own thoughts. His aggravation level seemed to be going up, but I didn't know why.

48

Out of curiosity I took a stab at the only reason that made any sense to me.

"I heard a rumor that you were going to be moving up in the world. Bigger and better things?"

Skip looked away. "Probably not now. Loren royally screwed up a chance I had with the city of Los Angeles. If the project had gone through, it would have looked great on my resume. Just the experience they were looking for, putting that kind of deal together, getting the funding." He put his hands on the desk, spreading his fingers and looking at them almost in fascination. "That's the way it goes." But I didn't hear any veracity in his voice.

Then he looked past me. I almost wanted to turn around and see who might be there. "I remember him," Skip said slowly, "sitting there, and these are his exact words: 'The only way you'll tear my store down is over my dead body.'"

Chapter 11
Tuesday Noon

Who would have thought Skip had such a flair for the dramatic? I had almost felt the ghost of Loren seated next to me.

The ghost of suicide Loren…or the ghost of murdered Loren?

Was Skip bitter enough to take Loren up on his own threat, that of being a dead body? How much had getting the job with the city of Los Angeles meant to him?

Thoughts leapfrogged over each other as I took the stairs to my office. Hard to put Skip into the role of murderer. Each of us is capable, another voice in my head said. Sudden anger, hitting someone who then died from the impact. Each of us could lose it for a second.

That wasn't true for Loren's murderer. I was looking for someone who planned the murder. Someone who knew Loren. Planning a murder and spur-of-the-moment anger leading to violence were a tad different. The courts thought so, too.

The murder was planned, and planned to look like suicide.

The murderer had to have the means to do it. That meant being strong enough to hoist Loren up and hold him there long enough to slip the noose around his neck to hang him. The murderer had to have a motive. At the moment, I seemed to have a surplus of people with motives. The murderer also had to have the opportunity. Who was around when Loren died?

Loren had offered the murderer a chance to do the deed by being in the store every Sunday morning. Before nine, regular as clock work, car in the parking lot, store door unlocked. A neon sign couldn't have done the job better.

What happened to the Sunday morning lady friend who usually arrived at nine?

Back at the office, I started on the mundane paperwork, glancing out of the window often, looking at the palm trees and the mountains which gave me a sense of peace. I realized that I'd been rushing everywhere, hardly taking time to smell the flowers.

I concentrated on the paperwork, my method of coping with thoughts too terrible to entertain. The firm in downtown Los Angeles, probably to justify my existence here in downtown Mirasol for the accountant's ledger, now was sending me everything related to Mirasol.

I mean everything. The firm had several lawyers, all with secretaries, paralegals, and other support staff at the downtown Los Angeles office. Here, only Audrey and I handled the deluge of files.

The cases included people suing the City for a variety of reasons, and vice versa. I dashed off notes of instruction to Audrey.

As the bulk of the paperwork was about to make its way off my desk to Audrey's, my thoughts slid to the Sunday morning lady friend. She arrived at nine...too early to be a regular churchgoer. The parking lot of the First Methodist Church, where she may have left her car, faced Nutwood, the side street running alongside Quon Lee's. Why did she park her car in the church's lot? She didn't want her car seen in the Balfour lot? Maybe she went to church afterwards.

Pushing the papers away from me, I stood up and stretched. I could walk from City Hall to the church, about five blocks.

So I marched off.

Nostalgia hit me as I saw my reflection in Queenie's Hair Stylist window as I walked past. The old name still there, faded, the shop empty. I patted my hair. I had worn it long for most of my life. Long and thick and very auburn with an energy all its own. Now it was short, still auburn and still with a will of its own. I thought about the people who called me carrot top or red. I hated that. Call me anything but that. Copper, russet, lots of names a whole lot more flattering.

Walking along, looking at the stores, I remembered how my girlfriends and I used to shop in these stores that were now boarded up. Especially Friday nights when we'd look in the store windows, talking, laughing, hoping all the time the cruising cars would stop, take us to Quon Lee's for a coke since that's where we were headed anyway. Once there, we all hoped that the love of our life at the time would stroll over and talk to us. There everyone could see everyone--those driving by, those sitting at the tables outside. The town still kept its old-fashioned atmosphere.

Nothing wrong with that, I guess. God, how times have changed. But the mating dance was still the same.

I laughed out loud. A woman walking by looked at me. Hope she didn't know I was the city attorney who was supposed to be a sane person.

Then I laughed mentally, smiling to myself at the mores of each age group. The laughter and the smile went away as I thought about the reason I was making this walking trip. It wasn't a stroll down memory lane; it was to find out about death.

I went past Quon Lee's diner to the corner, crossed Nutwood with the light, and turned left. Entering into the church parking lot, I tried to get into the mind of the Sunday morning lady friend. What would she be thinking?

I paced around the asphalt. No brilliant revelations.

What about the house across the alley with its side windows facing the back of Quon Lee's?

No answer to the doorbell.

Slipping back into the mode of the Sunday morning lady friend, I strode down the alley into the Balfour parking lot as though I were going into the store.

I saw the closed-up department store on the other side of Balfour's that Skip said had art and craft fairs on the weekend. No windows faced the lot so no chance of anyone from that building seeing anything.

On the east side, the side I was on, a cement block wall separated the backs of the houses from the parking lot. I could only see only the rooftops on Nutwood. No chance of a witness there. Unless it was a pigeon.

I walked along the side of the wall to the back of the parking lot. Bushes and trees and weeds entwined themselves into the steel fence. I peered through the gaps, not that there were many. Each house on the street behind the barrier had a backyard, so none of the homes were close to the fence.

Except one.

A window, almost against the fence, framed the face of a woman with white hair, and a pink shawl around her shoulders. I jumped back, startled, when I saw her, and then felt embarrassed as though I'd been caught listening at a keyhole. Almost as bad, window peeping. I looked back again wanting to give some indication that I was a harmless creature. She smiled, and waved. I waved back.

Then I hotfooted it out of the parking lot. Up Nutwood to the first street. Cremona. Left. I was practically running and quickly getting out of breath. I needed to exercise more. Pulling air into my lungs felt painful.

I walked along Cremona, looking down driveways. It took me a few minutes to find the right place.

The small house sat at the end of the cement driveway behind a larger house. I knocked on the door. The lady with the white hair and pink shawl seated in a wheelchair opened it. Introducing myself, I told her I worked for the city attorney's office and was just checking out a few things with regard to Balfour's, and asked if I could talk to her. I realized I didn't have any identification to show her other than my driver's license. My picture was hardly recognizable.

Would she let me, a stranger, into her home after I had peered into her window? But then I didn't look much like a serial killer.

"Would you like to come in for a cup of tea?" The woman swung her wheelchair aside as an invitation to enter, and indicated where to sit.

From where I perched on the chair, I watched as she carefully made tea, placed large cookies on a china plate, and set it on a tray along with silver spoons and linen napkins. I realized that the kitchen was built with everything at her level.

We sat at one end of the rectangular living room. Through the hedges, I had a view of the parking lot and the back of the Balfour store. My heart was racing. From the dash here or from anticipation?

"The police have already been here about it...about Mr. Balfour's death, you see," she said in answer to my question. "Took pictures, measured things. Even had a woman stand by the store just as she would if she were going in, and they wanted me to describe her. Testing my sight to be sure. Could I see what she wore and all that from here, they asked me, but as I told the young man in charge...let's see, I have his card right here." She wheeled to the window, pulled out a drawer under the telephone, and gave me the card.

Calvin L. Elkhart. Who else? I wanted to get my hands on him for not telling me about this. Young man? Then I realized the woman sitting opposite me must be at least eighty.

"I told the young man I couldn't distinguish features at that distance. It is a long way, but I do use these." She opened a cupboard under the window and pulled out binoculars.

Bingo.

"Have some chocolate chip cookies. I make them myself, you see. Real chocolate, baked from scratch." She smiled. I thought her face a perfect picture of what a grandmother should look like.

I shook my head at the cookies she offered.

"It's fun on Saturdays, everyone tries to park right by the entrance," she smiled. "Saw some boys one evening trying to break into the cars and called the police."

That's how Cal found out about her. He didn't even have to budge from his office to locate this witness. All he did was check the crime reports for Balfour's. And he'd find her name and address as a witness.

If I confronted him with not telling me about this information, he'd probably say he sent the report in the inter-office mail to me.

Right.

"They asked me what I saw that Sunday. Knew something happened, the paramedics and all," she said.

"What happened on other Sundays?"

"I told the young man she arrived at the same time. You could set your watch by her; 9:02. Always dressed up, like she was going to church. But I suppose she wanted to look nice for him," she said.

"What do you mean by that?" I asked.

"Well, my dear, I don't really know anything, but I do like to make up stories about the people who go into the store. I wonder about their lives. It was easy to do a story about the woman and

Mr. Balfour. Mr. Balfour always arrived first, you see. If he was there, the lights were on, and the door on the left unlocked. At least that's the one she always went in, and I never saw her use a key."

"Describe her to me."

The woman did, but it could fit any number of females—blonde hair, medium height, slender. Even Dottie, my manicurist, fit the description.

"I couldn't guess the age, my dear. He asked me if she might have dyed her hair or wore a wig, but I really couldn't tell. Are you sure you won't have a cookie?"

I shook my head, barely registering her question. "What did you tell the police you saw that Sunday?"

"Well that was it, you see. I wasn't watching the whole time. Usually nothing happens after she goes in. But what I did see was a little unusual."

"What do you mean by 'unusual'?" The house had warmed up. Or maybe it was the hot tea. I took off my jacket. I pushed back my hair, now beginning to feel warm and prickly around my face.

"I may have this mixed up a little, but it seems to me a car drove out the driveway and turned right on Main. Just then, a man walked from the alley and marched right up to the door like he knew it would be unlocked."

"What did he look like?"

"Taller than Mr. Balfour. I don't know how tall either of them were. I can only tell you where they came to on the door."

"On the door?"

"If you look at the door you'll see the white lines going across it. That's what I mean. Let me put the kettle on again. There's nothing like a fresh pot of tea."

I picked up the binoculars and looked at the doors through them. Square panes of glass divided by white wood. The doors appeared so close I could even see where they needed to be cleaned.

"Now, my dear, to answer your question about what he looked like." The woman wheeled back with the pot of tea on a tray on her lap. "The man had very light hair, perhaps grey, quite short. Thin. My father would say that one good wind would blow him away," she laughed, "and that's exactly the way he looked."

She poured more hot tea.

"The car that drove off," I said. "Did you see the person in it? Man? Woman?"

"Only saw the car. I don't know anything about cars except that it was a black one."

"You said you could tell how tall the men were from the level they reached on the door. Where did the woman reach?"

"That second pane of glass." I looked through the binoculars again. "Almost a pane shorter than Mr. Balfour."

"Did you tell the police this?"

"You mean about how tall? They didn't ask and I never thought about it until you mentioned it right now."

"Did you see anyone else that morning?"

"I saw Mr. Balfour's son go in—"

"Which one?"

"It's hard to tell those boys apart. I can't really say whether it was Bob or Eric, they look so much alike.

"What time?"

"About 9:30. And then a few minutes later the paramedics were there, and the police. Lots of people."

"What time did the woman get there? The same time?"

"Well, there you are my dear, I never saw her. At least she didn't come at her usual time. Because just about her usual time that tall, thin man came."

"The one with light hair?"

"That's right."

"So other people could have come and gone without you seeing them? Even the woman?"

"That's right, but as I said, the woman didn't come at her usual time." She offered me the plate.

"I think you'd better let the officer who left his card know what you remember about the woman's height."

"Oh, yes, I will. He told me to call him if anyone came by to ask me any questions."

Oh, no. I gasped involuntarily. I didn't want Cal to know I was investigating.

The old woman's gentle face looked stricken. Then she smiled. "I'm sure, my dear, he didn't mean every time someone dropped in for a chat and tea," she said, filling my cup again. "Have a chocolate chip cookie."

This time I took one. I took a bite. As I chewed, I decided these had to be best chocolate chip cookies I'd ever eaten. It almost drove every other thought out of my mind. Chocolate oozed into every crevice of my mouth. My mouth filled with chocolate saliva. They could be habit-forming.

It would be so easy to become addicted to the cookies, I might even move in.

Chapter 12
Tuesday Evening

That night there was a birthday party at The Granada, an old Mirasol restaurant still owned by descendants of the original land grant family.

Imagining what celebrations were like in the ranchero days wasn't hard. Even if you didn't know anyone when you arrived, you'd be an old friend by the time you left. Full of laughter, music and good food, the restaurant tries to replicate the early California hacienda hospitality.

Cal waved me over, so I slid in next to him in a booth. It was his hangout, I knew.

He had relayed a message through his department's secretary to Audrey inviting me to the party, as though embarrassed to ask me directly. I wondered who the party was for and, in particular, why I had been invited. But the invitation seemed a casual one as though a group of people were getting together and I was to join them. I had to admit that my social life was not awhirl, so I decided to attend.

I spotted Rachel dancing in the middle of the large, crowded floor. I couldn't see her partner, just a bunch of bobbing heads, bouncing to a fast Mariachi tune. The brassy sound of the trumpeters trilling those high notes was sheer heaven as far as I was concerned.

I tapped to the sound and watched the musicians and the dancers for a few minutes as I settled into the ambiance of the dark-paneled restaurant. When I turned to Cal, I noticed he wore what looked like his fifth Granada's Special Margarita in his eyes. Or it could have been his sixth. Thinking about all that lime juice gave me an acidic stomach. Brandy mixed with tequila wouldn't give me a good feeling either, but apparently it did so for Cal.

I took a gulp from the glass of water at my place.

"You know all about this stock fracas with the Balfours," Cal said with a seriousness around his mouth. "Explain it to me."

Is that why I had received the invitation? He couldn't admit that he wanted some information from me?

"What happened to 'hello' and 'how are you'?"

"That comes later."

Funny how I could look him right in the eye and smile back. "You want me to discuss the intricacies of corporate stock here?" I looked around the restaurant.

"Just the highlights."

Sort of the same summary I had wanted of Skip. In twenty words or less, tell me everything.

Stomping of feet in unison on the wooden dance floor caught my attention for a moment, then I went back to what I was saying. "The whole family owns stock," I said. "It's called a closely-held corporation, and no comments, please."

"Moi?" said Cal using an exaggerated motion to point to himself with one hand while the other held his drink in the air so that it rolled dangerously near the salted edge.

"It's like any other corporation," I said, "except that only family members can purchase stock or give it to other family members. However, the family has to vote on the distribution of the stock."

Cal nodded. He set his drink squarely on the table. We were working—his working voice turned on. "Heard old Mr. Balfour, Loren's father, voted against Win getting any even after she and Loren were married," he said. "Win wasn't flesh and blood. Even though she was the mother of old Mr. Balfour's grandkids."

"I haven't read the minutes of the stockholders' meetings. They have to keep and file them even though the stock is owned only by family members."

"Not known for being Mr. Nice Guy." Cal paused as though thinking about it all. He grabbed his glass and drank off the rest of his margarita, then yelled, "Garcon," waving the over-sized glass, still salt-encrusted on one side.

An old-time waiter, Joseph Bydgoszcz "from the town and the province of the same name in Poland" he always told first-timers,

59

came over. He now cultivated a very Zapata moustache. "Reddy for the brandee?"

"Si," said Cal, flourishing part of his Spanish vocabulary to the Pole. Then he turned to me. "Where were we?" he said.

"I'll spare you all the gory details and just tell you that Loren had the controlling interest. That is, he had the most shares."

"With the twins, Eric and Bob, and Missy owning some. Win, also?"

"Very good, Cal," I said. "Yes, Loren gave Win some more stock after his father died."

"Like an 'up yours' to the old man who was now in his grave," said Cal.

"That, or an 'I love you' to Win."

Interesting that we had different takes on Loren's gift of stock to Win, different interpretations of Loren's action. It sure revealed a lot about our personalities.

"Maybe. Maybe he should have said it before." Cal watched as Joseph set down the globe of brandy. It looked like a triple. Cal gave him a smile, the one that had dazzled all his teachers in high school. Joseph nodded.

"Next," Cal said turning back to me.

"Sheila, Loren's sister, was in an insane—"

"She died last year."

"I know. While she was alive, Loren controlled her shares as he was her guardian. Her will, which was written before she was committed, left her stock to Missy. Now Loren no longer had a controlling interest. So he sued the estate, saying her will was invalid—"

"Loren's the one who committed her."

I nodded. "If the will had been declared invalid, the stock would go to Loren as her closest relative But it wasn't declared invalid, so Missy inherits."

"Missy?" Cal's eyes showed surprise. "Is that funny, or is that funny? So Missy, her niece, got the goods." He laughed again and took a gulp of the brandy. I could almost taste it in my own throat, burning. I was getting drunk just from the fumes. I took another big drink of water.

"If you want to laugh harder, Cal, Missy also gets quite a bit of money from Sheila's will."

"Whard'shegitthafrom?" That's what Cal's words sounded like to me.

"Old Mr. Balfour, Sheila's father, Mr. Not-So-Nice as you called him, wanted her to have a good dowry. Anyhow, it was invested well, so there's quite a bit."

"How much—never mind." He waved his hand as though to push the words off the table. A small smile crept onto his face. I paused for a minute, wondering if Missy might be in the old girlfriend pool. Or maybe the current one. She had just come back from several years in East Africa. Alone.

I wondered if that's what he wanted me to think.

"So what happens with Loren's death? His stock?"

"His will followed California law exactly. Win gets half, and the other half is divided equally among his three children, Eric, Bob, and Missy."

He barely nodded, getting to the sloppy stage—napkin on the floor, jacket sliding off the leather seat, guacamole on his shirt.

"A nice neat way of solving a family squabble," Cal said.

"You mean Loren committing suicide?"

Cal's eyes were dark. "No, I mean Loren's death." With that he threw back the rest of the brandy.

Chapter 13
Wednesday 5 to 7 P.M.

My social life certainly was picking up speed.

The opening of the New Far East Bank, combined with a fund raiser for the YMCA, drew a large crowd. Lots of chamber and Y members. Since it had been well publicized, there was only a sardine-size space for each person in the bank. A fire marshal's delight, however I noticed his boss, the fire chief, nibbling on hors d'oeuvres and talking to a city council member who, I was sure, was one of the investors in the new bank. Ah, the intricacies of relationships in a small town.

I moved away from the teller's cage, now the bar, with my gin and tonic made by Ed of toupee fame. I looked over the crowd and had to smile as everyone seemed so happy. Contagious.

Kirby caught my eye and wove his way over with Lars in tow. I mentally groaned—no escape. It wasn't because of Kirby; it was Lars.

"Have you met Lars?"

I said, "Yes."

Lars blinked.

I had met him at least four times over the years, and Kirby had introduced us each time. I hoped he did it more for Lars' short-term memory loss than for mine. He seemed to want Lars to mingle, but it was obvious to me that Lars only wanted to stick by Marti's side and only attended public functions because Marti went. I sipped my drink and pondered the fact that Marti was now in the hospital. Then I tried to think pleasant thoughts. I could tell Ed hadn't spared the gin.

"Did you know Lars lifts weights? He can now bench press...how many pounds is it?"

I figured Kirby knew.

Lars answered with a number that was impressive, even to me who knew only that a bench press was an instrument of torture. He was bald and came up to my shoulder. He looked like I felt; we'd both rather be doing something else. Like walking on hot coals barefoot.

I reflexively looked down at Lars' shoulders, arms covered with a long-sleeved white shirt.

"Tell her about the time you lifted the VW off that man," Kirby said with anticipation as though he'd never heard the story before. Kirby's forehead glistened. The air conditioning blasted out cold air, but the temperature remained Sahara-like.

I looked back at Lars. "Oh yeah," he said as though trying to remember the exploit. And then he did, and his mental tape recorder kicked in, and off he went with the story, storytelling almost as well as Kirby.

"And he jacks up the car see...a little VW bug. Then for some reason he crawls under it, and like kicks the jack so it goes off, and the car comes down on him. Wham." He hit his right fist into his palm.

I almost spilled my drink in surprise at his animation.

While Lars talked he watched the floor as through that's where the action took place.

"Was he hurt?"

"Uh, uh. So it comes down on him, and see, I'm standing across the street, just happened to be watching. So then I go across the street, see, 'cause this guy needs help."

So did I. I glanced around to see if someone would rescue me.

Lars nodded several times at the picture on the floor. Maybe his mental tape had stuck. I could only hope.

No such luck.

"So this other guy comes over, and I says get ready to pull him out 'cause I'm going to lift the car, so I did. Knew I could do it." He relived his movements, showing how he lifted the car, taking the stance, knees bent, wriggling his body, and then getting a good grip.

"So I lifted it, see, and then the other guy drags him out. Then I put the car down."

I was at a loss for words. How to give this deed its proper due?

"That's really something. How much did the car weigh?"

"The car weighed a good, maybe a good two thousand pounds, but see I'm not lifting the whole thing, only one corner of it."

"So you mean you were only lifting five hundred pounds? That's four corners into two thousand."

He didn't smile, just kept his eyes on the floor.

I could tell that ended the show, nothing more to be seen on the floor, and Kirby skillfully moved him on. I shook my head. Now what was that all about? Trying to make Lars feel important?

Mentally my eyes crossed. Maybe I was getting old and cranky when my time was wasted in moments that I didn't enjoy, particularly when I came to an event that should be fun.

Why was my blood pressure rising? Because he bored me? Because I saw no point to why Kirby wanted him to tell me that story? Why me? Because I wouldn't walk away? I looked around. Not many people here would walk away. They were all nice people, courteous, patient and other things that Boy Scouts espoused.

My knowledge of Lars was mostly seeing him with Marti. Lars seemed to be some sort of man Friday around the house. I wasn't sure exactly what he did or why he lived with them.

"I've got some really good info," Cal whispered behind me, interrupting my thoughts. His plastic glass was filled to the top with amber. No ice.

"About what?"

"Shhh," he sprayed it out. When he moved his hand, liquid spilled out of his glass onto the new burgundy carpet. Would the alcohol bleach it? How many drinks had Ed given him? "I'll tell you tomorrow," he said.

"Give me a hint. I can't stand the suspense."

"It's got to do with..." He looked like he was having trouble focusing both his eyes and his mind.

"Come on, big guy, let's go home, I've had a long day," a voice said behind me. "Hi, Rachel," I said.

"You don't do anything...all day...file your nails," Cal grinned at her, eyes blinking and watering as though struggling to focus.

Deja vu.

"Yeah, well, that makes me tired." Rachel winked at me. I

smiled back. "Let's go."

"Okay, Mommy." She took hold of his arm and gently tugged him toward the door. Half of his drink had gone over the side.

What did he have to tell me? Now I'd have to wait until tomorrow.

Chapter 14
Friday 6 P.M.

The dream again. The bad one.

The dream, based on the reality of the past, is that Nate Goodfellow and I are at work in Morrie & West, a fancy-schmancy law firm in Century City. Civil law, no criminal, which is why I'm there after ten years in the D.A.'s office. I also have a newly-dead husband.

Lester Barrone, the senior of the senior partners, always sprouting bow ties, asks us to take over a small criminal matter for a long-time client. Read: lucrative client.

I've been there a month. I'm there because they do no criminal work. I'm burned out on murder and mayhem. I never want to see another dead body, kilo of marijuana, or crime of any kind. I've had it, recognizing that I'm trying to navigate a perilous mental balance after losing my best friend-husband.

No matter that Lester knows none of this. And if he did, would it matter?

The bow tie of yellow polka dots, the color psychedelic bright, is burned in my mind.

Nate and I are the only ones with criminal experience. Nate and I are the newest members of the staff.

I start to wonder at that point if I, a token woman, and Nate, a token black man, and homosexual but no one knows that, were hired solely as the token whatever. Paranoia comes easy after all the bad guys I came in contact with in the D.A.'s office. I say none of this to Nate. I don't know him well enough yet to bad mouth the firm in any way.

He's been a federal criminal attorney for five years and I get the impression he'd like to see another side of life. But I'm not sure exactly where he's at mentally.

When the file comes, we sit at the conference table in front of the floor-to-ceiling window in my office and read it with increasing depression—it deepening as the day, sun and sky becomes more joyous.

Leroy's his name, but we call him Sonnyboy. At twenty years old has more arrests than anybody his age should have, all for rough stuff. But no convictions and no time served. A pattern emerges that makes the back of my neck prickle. No witnesses, nor any victims, ever testify, so Sonnyboy walks. Sonnyboy walks all the time.

He takes care of everything by intimidating witnesses. That's what Nate and I read between the lines. Nasty stuff. And he's our client.

The juvenile record is sealed, but we guess at its contents. In a way, we don't want to know. We don't want to know how bad it is. We guess pretty bad. Meanwhile Sonnyboy sits in the slammer as an adult for big time stuff, shooting a male Caucasian in a small mom-and-pop store and killing him—hard not to do with a shotgun at close range.

A store video shows the entire crime going down. At that point Nate and I just want to close the file folders and get Sonnyboy to plea bargain, maybe take life imprisonment if we were ever able to convince the D. A. to offer it. However, we soon find out plea bargaining isn't an option Daddy will agree to. We haven't counted on having to deal with Daddy.

Our primary concern, now, is keeping the video from being introduced as evidence. If the judge allows the jury to see it, we figure they will convict him in the time it takes them to walk to the jury room, vote, and file back to their seats in the jury box.

Nate and I have been in too many criminal trials.

When the jury's verdict comes in, it's hard to say who is more surprised—Annabelle Lane, the prosecuting attorney, or Nate and I.

We win.

Fast forward.

I'm back at the office after lunch. A big basket of fruit and champagne from Sonnyboy's Daddy arrives. Nate comes in at the same time. We decide to celebrate.

Nate's about to open the champagne.

Sonnyboy walks in.

Shotgun. Pulls it out of his baggy pant leg, like he's taking a hanky out to blow his nose.

He points it at Nate and says something. The blood is pounding in my head. I ask him, "What did you say?"

Sonnyboy swings the shotgun toward me. Nate yells at him. Sonnyboy swings the shotgun back.

Boom.

Boom.

Nate's head explodes like a watermelon.

Boom.

A large, red flower blossoms on his off-white shirt.

Behind Nate, the glass shatters like instant frost.

Sonnyboy turns to me with his shotgun.

He has a smile on his face like a religious experience washes over him.

I throw up. All over the desk. It just pools on the top and runs down the sides, all over my suit and shoes. Red Cabernet on white paper. Lobster. The stuff keeps coming out of me like I'm a fountain.

No more smiles on Sonnyboy. Disgusted. He backs out of the office and vanishes.

That's the dream, the nightmare, the reality. I was stuck in it. Over and over.

The buzzing blended into the dream. Alarm bells.

Not my clock alarm.

I fumbled for the cordless phone, almost knocking it off the nightstand.

Without preamble she said, "Cal's in deep do-do up to his eyeballs. I need your help."

Rachel.

"What happened?"

"He wouldn't let me drive us home last night. No sense arguing with him when he's in a mood."

I could hear Rachel pull on a cigarette and exhale the smoke. My stomach did a roll. I groped for the light and the clock.

"We pull up to a stop sign, and there's a patrol car in front of us. Cal says, 'Hey that's my old buddy, Bollins, I'm just going to give him a little nudge in the rear end. I gotta tell you, it was no nudge. We're talking damage to their police car, and I can hardly wait to get an estimate on our Mercedes. Anyhow, they jump out of their car, guns drawn—I mean, after all, somebody's just rammed their police car. Cal is reaching for his wallet. Of course they see he's wearing a gun, and I had to yell at them 'He's a police officer.' They literally yank him out of the car, see his badge and his pager—that's probably what really convinced them—and they finally hear what I'm trying to tell them."

Another pull on the cigarette, another exhale.

I looked at the clock. 6 a.m.

"It wasn't Bollins, and it wasn't even a Mirasol car. We weren't even in Mirasol. It happened right there on the strip of county property that crosses Main. They want to give him professional courtesy and all that. But they look at the back end of their car, and I figure they're thinking how are they going to explain that."

Pull, and exhale.

"Cal says he'll pay for it, and he gets his wallet out and starts waving hundred dollar bills around. They tell him to let me drive, but he keeps saying no. Then he gets back in the car and starts to take off for real. That does it for them. They put him in the patrol car and tell me to drive home."

I got a bad feeling in the middle of my chest as I listened to Rachel.

"They tell me they're going to let him sleep it off at the station. To make a long story short, word gets to the chief. Which doesn't make her too happy, needless to say—you know how she's been on Cal's case—so she calls up the sheriff's department and asks them to deliver Cal to her office pronto. That's like at five this morning. So they do."

I looked at the clock again. Over an hour ago. News travels fast in a small town.

"Lord only knows what the chief said to him. Hard to believe they were once partners."

Rachel stayed silent for a moment. I tried to read the silence on the line, but couldn't. My mind slowly took it all in. I knew there was a bottom line to what she told me, and it didn't have a happy face on it.

"In other words he's going to be drying out for thirty days in a detox center, but it ain't going to be the Betty Ford Clinic. He won't be able to go anywhere or see anybody. I know you two are working on a case...hell, I just had to tell someone." Her voice is choked up. Clicks sounded as though she was flipping the lighter, firing up another cigarette.

My mind labored into the next gear. "He can't see anybody?" I said. "You mean no visitors?" It's the first thing that came out of my mouth.

"Only me and close family. Which around here is only me."

"Rachel—"

"It's okay. I wanted to ask you to let me know what happens. I mean anything that I should know."

"Yes, I will."

"Okay, thanks. I've got to go now, get ready for work," she said.

For the first time in a long spell I put on a sweat suit and running shoes—new orange ones—and set out for a run around the park three blocks away.

My routine from long ago. Plan my day. Think about priorities. After Ted, I'd slacked off. And then when Nate...
I loped along, at least that's the way I pictured myself. There were probably other words to describe my gait, but not as positive. As I ran, I thought about Cal. I wouldn't be able to find out what he was going to tell me. Thirty days. And Deb would be pushing for a progress report. Didn't matter that she just had a baby.

Interesting that Rachel should say Cal and I were working on a case together. Made me wonder what he had said to her. Made me wonder what she thought—another girl in a red dress?

A lot of things could happen in thirty days.

Someone would be replacing Cal on all his cases. I thought about the possibilities. I came up with two. Garbage Mouth and Mr. Personality.

Back at the office, Audrey handed me the results of the tissue report with a shake of her head. "Translation of all this gobbley-gook is that it's all Loren's tissue," she said.

Suddenly the vivid image of Loren dangling there, trying to pull at the cord choking him to death, filled my head.

My knees buckled and my stomach fell about forty floors. Skin tissue. I took the report and staggered into my office, plunking down on my chair. My stomach roiled and spasmed. For a moment I thought its contents were going to be elevated by express, and I looked around for the wastepaper basket.

My foot kicked it and I heard again in my memory the shotgun blasts, double-barreled, that shattered Nate and the window twenty-three stories above Avenue of the Stars, and sprayed me with his skin and tissue.

Everything was up and came out just as it had that day.

Chapter 15
Friday 7 P.M.

Quon Lee left a message on my machine. "The Coalition of Ten," I heard him laugh slightly as he said the name. "We meet tonight at 7:30. Corky and Mary Cordero's. Everybody very pleased you attend."

Come 7 p.m., I slapped on a little more makeup to cover the still-dark crescents under my eyes and the prison pallor of my face, then set off.

I had to get back into a routine. I had to run every day. Set a schedule. Tomorrow I would sit down and write one up. I felt like my life was out of control. Not good. I was working more than twenty hours. I had to remember this was only a part-time job, which is what I wanted.

What had I planned to do with the rest of my time when I made that decision? I wondered what I had been thinking two months ago. Had I wanted a part-time job because I didn't want to handle anything as strenuous as going to work every day? Had I been thinking about staying in bed all the time? Or was I just thinking I had no more energy, no more fight, no more patience for the stupid things people did to other people? I couldn't remember what I'd been thinking. Two months was a long time ago.

Mary Cordero greeted me in her usual affable manner and pressed a drink of Mexican brandy into my hand. "It's Don Pedro Reserva Especial," she said. "I went down to see my sister in Mexico City. She's really getting high-falutin' these days. Her husband's been appointed consul to some country. You should see their house. Wow. And does she look good. Corky's real sorry she's not the one who came up here instead of me."

"Don't you believe her, Jo. Mary's just trying to start trouble as usual."

I laughed. Corky belonged to the original land grant settlers from Mexico who traced their residency in California back to the 1700s.

"Keep me out of this," I said. "I don't want to be responsible for the end of a forty-something-year old marriage." Not that I, or anyone, could be, but I still changed the subject. "What's the lineup tonight? Who's coming?"

"Here's the list we got from the Planning Department." Corky handed the printout to me.

MAIN STREET PROJECT

ADDRESS	BUSINESS	OWNER
112	(Beauty Salon)	Kirby Hawkins
120	Supermarket	Mary and Corky Cordero
134	Medical building	Warren Anderson
148	(Jewelry store)	Probate/Judge Julie J. Smith
152	(Women's clothing)	Kirby Hawkins
160	(Men's clothing)	" "
172	(Shoe store)	Charles Quinn
184	(Department store)	*Wing Dag Bat
191	Furniture store	Balfour Family
198	Diner	Quon Lee

( ) indicates business is no longer operating
* weekend art and craft sales only

"Everyone comes," Mary said, "except the judge on the probate, and we let her know what we're doing. Wing comes, but his English is as good as my Korean, so he brings his daughter. Head of her class at Mirasol High and cute as can be. If my grandson knew she was coming over tonight..."

Kirby came in first, pumping hands with both of them and then with me.

"How's Marti doing?" I asked as he clasped my hand.

"Fine, fine. Going to the hospital after this to see her. Well, hello there, Mr. Bat." Ten seconds for Marti.

"What I started to tell you," said Mary, "was that Charlie Quinn doesn't come, not that we've been meeting all that long. We finally tracked him down. Lives in Palm Springs in an old house trailer out in the middle of nowhere. Probably got a ton of money, wouldn't you say, Kirby?"

"Could be," he said.

"Never know it to see him, got a beard down to his knees practically, all white, looks like one of those old prospectors. Real sweet on Sheila Balfour. Remember that Kirby? You were too, come to think of it." She elbowed him.

Kirby looked uncomfortable, but he laughed. "You better not tell Marti. It's taken me all these years to convince her Sheila and I were just friends."

"I don't believe it took you that long to convince her," said Mary.

"No one hears from Charlie?" I asked her as I watched Kirby move into the living room, and Eric and Bob arrived. Mary's greetings were subdued. What could she say about their father's death? She turned back to me as the twins went into the living room also, and I heard them being greeted by the others.

"Charlie's paying property taxes and getting whatever licenses he has to have like the rest of us. We mail him stuff, planning department mails him stuff. None of it comes back, so if he reads it, he knows what's going on," said Mary.

Warren Anderson next.

Corky ushered us in with the rest. "All right, you old duffers," he said in his emcee voice. "I'm calling this meeting to order." Corky hit a spoon on the side of his coffee mug.

"We're not down the tubes yet, guys, so we still have to keep fighting. Now that's the good news. The bad news is the city's going to abandon the Main Street Project after the stay unless," he paused for drama, "we get our act together.

"So why we're meeting is to decide what we want to do. Then Quon Lee here will tell his lawyer son, Sammy, and Sammy's going to try to get it for us. Now let me bring you up to date—"

"The city's at fault. They killed Loren." I didn't have to look in his direction to know the voice came from Warren Anderson, the town's political gadfly. No one said anything in response to Warren's remark. All too typical of him, as though arguing was a way for him to relate to people.

"We've got to all stick together," said Corky. "We can't be accusing the city of this and that and then still try to negotiate with them. Are you with us, Warren? Part of the group?"

Warren became unsettled with everyone watching him. "I want what everybody else wants: no boarded-up windows." His voice lowered and then fell to a mutter-level decibel.

"Who else? Anybody else feel differently?" Corky kept control of the meeting.

Some made comments, some asked questions, but they seemed to be in accord. They wanted the project to be a reality just as Skip had predicted to me.

"Before we go any further, there's one thing we'd better tell you," said Bob.

There was instant silence. Even Warren stopped muttering. A collective in-drawn breath. Did this mean they were going to follow Loren's lead and try to stop the project? I imagined hearts beat in dread as to what Bob might say. He didn't look very happy.

"We can't find Dad's stock certificates."

Everyone looked at each other. Only the whisper of Wing Dag Bat's daughter translating to him broke the silence. He seemed as puzzled as the rest as everyone looked from Bob to Eric.

"Drop the other shoe, Bob. What does that mean?" said Corky.

"It means we can't show 100% ownership."

"It means," said Eric softly, "we can't sell the store, can't join with everybody, without the certificates. Without the actual certificates, we won't have a majority vote."

I did a mental double-take at this news. The stock certificates were missing? I immediately wondered what that had to do with Loren's death. A motive? For whom?

"Let me ask you this question," Corky said, "if you had the stock would you vote to sell?"

"Sure," Bob and Eric answered without hesitation.

A collective sigh of relief. I felt the tension in the room dissipate.

"How does your father's will distribute the stock?" I asked.

Eric looked at me, ran fingers through his hair. "We couldn't find a will."

"By California law," I said, "half goes to Win and the other half will be divided among the three of you."

"We can't find the stock certificates," said Eric. "We have to have them before we can sell."

"You mean without the stock certificates, you ain't got nothing to sell?" Heads all swiveled to Warren.

Eric and Bob nodded, sadly I thought.

Silence for a moment, even after Wing Dag Bat's daughter's low voice stopped.

"Anybody for some Don Pedro Reserva Brandy?" said Mary. "Looks like we all need it."

Chapter 16
Saturday 9 A.M.

"Hi, honey. Oh, the roses are gorgeous," Mother said.

I was surprised to see her standing, even on crutches. I handed her the flowers, and she fumbled with the crutches, then buried her face in the bouquet, taking a deep breath.

Her color was better, her hair neater. "I'd go for a walk with you down the hall, but I just got back." She sat down in the chair, leaving me the side of the bed. "Ah, I'm still out of breath."

"How are you?"

"Fine. I'll improve magnificently as soon as I escape from this institution. These are so awkward." She indicated the white cast and the crutches. "After I get out of here, I'm going to get on the hospital board and change a few things around here. Champagne for dinner."

I laughed in spite of myself. Knowing Mother, it could happen. Then she gave me detailed instructions about plant watering and clothes she wanted me to bring. I listened with an attentive and, what I hoped was a pleasant look on my face. This time my irritation level was low as I had a payback in mind.

I didn't have to remember anything--she had it all written down. Now for my payback.

"I need some information from your real estate database about who owns what," I said.

"I can't help with that until I get out of here."

We sat for a moment in silence then she said, "I suppose you could use my computer. Just call me up when you get there, and I'll walk you through it. But be careful, everything is very sensitive." I wasn't sure if she meant the information or the computer. I guessed the latter.

Her impatience remained controlled. Maybe she thought that by helping me she would get her plants watered and her clothes delivered sooner. Her plants were in less danger if I did nothing. It all gave me a great excuse to cut the visit short and take off for Mother's place.

With the telephone on my shoulder, I listened to Mother's instructions on how to access her unique home-grown program on her museum-piece computer.

"I want to find out what else everyone in the Main Street Project owns," I said.

Under her direction I keyed in their names along with their DBA, business names that she gave me.

She had devised her own computer commands and I would never have been able to access the file without her help. I started to take notes on her instructions in case I had to do it again on my own. Who knew when she would be this compliant again? But after awhile my notes melded into scribbles. I gave that up.

I had counted on the fact that she had more information about real estate property changing hands in one place than I'd find anywhere else.

I wasn't disappointed as the screen filled with facts and figures and charts. The members of the coalition all owned more property than I thought, in addition to what they owned as part of the Main Street Project.

No question that if the project went through, all of their other properties would rise in value considerably. Something they must have been thinking about for a long time.

I wondered why the renovation of downtown had taken so long. Money, probably. Now they had grants from the federal government that hadn't existed in the past. I could ask these questions of Mother, and probably get the answer, but right now I didn't want to get her off the track of guiding me through the program. The computer was so old it almost clunked from one task to the next. Her zippy new one was in her office. The information on this one was not something she wanted to share with anyone.

"You can print out the list, but don't use up all my paper." There was a light note in her voice, but she was probably serious. I almost wanted to look to see if the paper was vellum or parchment or some expensive stuff from Venice. I needn't have looked; she was just being herself by saying that.

While the printer hummed away—actually it crackled as though munching on the paper that went through it—printed pages come out, Mother said, "Delbert's arranging for an ambulance to take me home the day after tomorrow. I can hardly stand the wait. I guess you could say I can hardly stand anyway." She laughed.

You'll miss everyone waiting on you, I thought. At least your plants here won't be dead by then. The plant god was looking after them.

"I simply can't bear the smell here. I have a headache all the time. Sinuses. Something in the vents. I've been sprinkling Chanel No. 5 around, but it doesn't seem to help. That's another of the things I'm going to change."

I pictured the new edict when she got on the hospital's board. Chanel and champagne. Great slogan. Hey, I might even go to that hospital. Come on printer, go faster. It was much newer than her computer.

"I'm going to burn all the clothes I had on when they brought me in here. I'd love to soak in a bubble bath as soon as I get home." She sighed, "But I can't for a while." I pictured her looking at her cast-covered leg.

For a second, I thought she was going to ask me to start running the water, then stay to help her keep her leg out of the tub. I held my breath. But her next words were on a different track.

"This place has Legionnaire's Disease in the air conditioning, I'm sure. I've told Delbert, but he just laughs at me. I have to be nice to him because I want out of here."

I had enough of her voice in my ear. It went all soft and furry when she talked about a man.

And besides, the printer had stopped. Maybe it was out of paper, but I was out of patience. Something else I'd inherited from my mother.

"How do I exit?" At this point I didn't care if she thought that a double entendre.

Bad enough her plants might die with me in proximity, but I didn't want to kill her computer program, too.

I might need it again.

Interesting reading. Kirby was the last of the group. As the page for him came out I grabbed the sheets. I jammed them into a file folder. But the printer kept going. Had I hit the print button for two copies of everything? Or worse, more? Was I going to use up all her paper after all? For a moment I just stood there watching the copies come out as though I was looking at some unstoppable beast. Should I pull the plug?

When I looked at the copies, they were all new pages. In all, five for Kirby. Property in the area. I glanced over the addresses. He must have inherited some of it from his father, judging from the purchase dates.

This from a man who wore suits that looked like they'd been bought when there was a sale on at the local thrift shop.

I held the file folder in my hand for a moment like an unexploded bomb.

What did it all mean? Anything? Nothing?

I took a quick tour around the house, looking at the plants. Most of them were African violets. Nothing was wilting, and they all seemed happy and cheerful, so I left them alone. I'm sure they sighed with relief when I left.

Chapter 17
Later

Long ago—actually two months after the coroner had zipped up what was left of Nate, my law firm colleague, in a body bag—I had walked out of Morrie & West, went home, crawled into bed, pulled the duvet over my head, and stayed there for a week. When I realized I was going to live despite my trauma, I pushed off the duvet and climbed out of bed like a sick ninety-year old.

I had worked in downtown Los Angeles for the district attorney's office and in Century City for the law firm of Morrie & West, but my home had always been in Mirasol. So why not really come home, employment-wise?

I had checked out who handled the legal business for Mirasol. Mirasol and other small cities didn't have a full-time city attorney. All the legal work was done by law firms specializing in municipal law. And there weren't many of them.

Paging through the Martindale-Hubbell directory I could find all the law firms listed, the kind of law each practiced, and all the lawyers who worked there.

Municipal law meant no criminal work. Just the county suing the city for toxic waste in the sewers, and the railroad. Ditto, for misuse of its right-of-way. Wonderfully quiet and sedate work that my soul salivated for. Bore me to sleep, please. I checked all the firms and the cities they served. And there it was. Mirasol.

No long hours, no freeways. Instead I could walk to work. I could get involved in Mirasol's community activities like the chamber of commerce, the YMCA, the Red Cross, with nothing more exciting than the Chinese New Year Festival and parade, nothing louder than the firecrackers. I might even be able to face spending an entire evening at home. Alone.

Maybe the gods would smile on me again. Looking down the

roll of attorneys on the staff of the firm that did Mirasol's legal work, I saw the name, Deborah Macklin Schwab.

Bingo.

We had gone to law school together. She would never win the 'easiest person in the world to get along with' award, but I figured I could last a whole telephone conversation with her while I begged for a job.

The gods were smiling. My timing couldn't have been better. She had just received yet another complaint from the new city manager about the level of service. Her comments could never be printed in a family newspaper.

Since losing a city was not good form, and since it was a small world and city managers talked to each other, the firm had to do something. Deb had to do some damage control.

As if my timing weren't good enough on that level, it was even better on another, for Deb was experiencing her first labor pain. Labor pain as in maternity.

"Here I am, Deb, hire me," I told her. "You can even call me at home. I live three minutes away from City Hall." I think that put the deal over the edge. Immediate response at no extra cost. The conversation ended with her gasp as another contraction hit her. Just like her to wait until the last minute.

The next day, with burgundy leather briefcase in hand, I went to City Hall to introduce myself as their new legal representative. Gilbert and I exchanged pleasantries. We knew each other from city functions. He'd bought his home from Mother. He was dashing off, he said, so didn't have time to say all that he might have wished to say. Or maybe he was just reserving judgment. Knowing someone socially is different from working with them. At least I was on the scene. Someone he could verbally bash in person if it came to that.

I took a look at the physical office—a cubicle of dark wood. Being confined in there for a period longer than a coffee break would definitely be depressing. As bad as Balfour's stockroom, only smaller. Was this the way the city viewed their legal counsel? I looked around, then opened the adjoining door to the conference room.

Ah ha!

Windows made up parts of the north and east walls which gave me a view of the San Gabriel Mountains. Light filled the room and my life. Bookcases of legal books lined one wall. Palm trees across the street added a lacy pattern to the bottom of the mountains. Not another sight like it in the world, and all mine. I plunked my briefcase down on the large table in the library cum conference room.

I decided it couldn't get much better, job-wise, than this. I could join the regulars for breakfast at the Pine Coffee Shop, walk to work, and say 'hello' to people on the way, people I had known all my life.

I was home.

Yesterday I had called Brendan, the office manager at Morrie & West. It was time to formally resign, and sever our short relationship. I tried not to think about that last afternoon there.

According to Brendan, the firm planned to keep me on the books as being 'on leave' until I decided to return.

"I'm not coming back, Brendan. I quit," I told him again.

"Three months," Brendan said, "and then I'm supposed to call you, see how much more time you want, with the implication that your leave can be extended very easily."

Since I'd given up swearing, and Brendan was a nice person whom I liked a lot, I said, "Listen to my lips, Brendan, I'm definitely not coming back, so put me on leave forever for all I care."

"This is a paid leave, my dear. Milk it."

"They're going to keep paying me?"

"Yes, oh dense one, I'll be sending you a check every pay period while the royalty here does damage control."

"I'm not saying I can't use the money, but I don't want to have anything to do with them."

"Confidentially," Brendan said in a voice so low I could barely hear him, "and I didn't tell you this. Certain people are worried that you're going to sue their proverbial pants off and everything that's in them—and for some of them that's not much. The partners will prepare a nice settlement package for you. That is, when your leave is up."

"Settlement? You mean like in severance pay, or like an

insurance company settlement?"

"Nooo, my dear, like in off-the-top settlement."

"Brendan, you mean it's coming out of the partners' profits?" I heard the incredulous note in my voice.

"My, aren't we a smart girl today. We're talking big bucks. That's why you should continue your leave. As it is, you have another month."

I could picture Brendan at his desk, his back to the view of downtown Los Angeles, tall and thin, in his mid-thirties with friendly blue eyes and nice looking in a boyish way. Considering the sound of his voice, he probably had a big smile on his face. But then, maybe he didn't.

I realized he had a motive to look after me, because looking after me was what he was doing. Nate had been his friend. Was he drawing out a little revenge for Nate? That was the only motivation I could guess that he had.

Very interesting news, but I kept in mind that Brendan's first loyalty was to the firm. After all, they were paying him handsomely to keep the office running smoothly, which he did well. I didn't tell him all the thoughts that were scuttling about like lizards in my mind.

"Tell them to send me a big settlement check."

"First the leave, my dear. Then the settlement. I'll drop a few words to keep their horror level high."

I laughed. I couldn't picture Lester Barrone, the senior of the senior partners, in any state of horror.

"I'll be back in touch," Brendan said. "And if I don't talk to you before, Happy Halloween."

Chapter 18
Saturday 10 A.M.

Next on my agenda was Charlie Quinn, a Main Street business owner who didn't attend the meetings.

That meant Palm Springs, so I packed an overnight bag in case I didn't feel like the two-hour drive home.

In Palm Springs, or rather outside the city limits, I found Charlie's trailer. One young tree tried to shelter the old Airstream. Neither looked permanent.

The scene was exquisite, though. There was desert sand all around, mountains in back silhouetted in brown against the blue sky. Absolute quiet. I savored it for a moment.

I knocked on the screen door. It reverberated tinily.

I heard a movement inside and felt him watching me. "Charlie?"

"Get away!"

I jumped back.

"Get away from here! I've got my shotgun ready, and I'll shoot through this door if I have to!"

Shotgun. Nate's bloodied body came to mind. I broke out into a cold sweat, my mind numb. I jerked back, stumbled, and fell. Blank spots in my vision again. I lay in the dusty sand for a moment feeling everything turn to ice. I expected tremors to start reverberating through my body as they had during the nights afterwards, but nothing happened. Just coldness.

And then I used the password. "Mary Cordero told me to look you up."

The door opened.

"Why didn't you say so right off? Did you hurt yourself?" His voice had lost its threatening edge.

"No. I'm Jo Peters from Mirasol. You're Charlie Quinn?" No

long beard. His hair was short and white, his cheeks and chin pale, forehead tanned. I looked at him taking it all in as though he was an apparition.

"You say you know Mary Cordero?"

"Right. And Corky. I work for the city attorney's office. Live in Mirasol, in fact I was born there," I said talking quickly and nervously, my derriere still parked in the sand.

"Left forty years ago. You weren't even born then."

Not only wasn't I born, my parents hadn't even met.

"Yes, I know."

He set the shotgun down next to the door. "Here, let me help you up. Got some coffee brewing. Want some?"

"Sure."

"Come on in then."

As I passed the upended shotgun, the barrels looked like the size of the mouths of cannons. I tried to keep my eyes away from them.

Inside he gestured to the booth-style table, and poured tin mugs of coffee.

I talked about the Coalition of Ten, asked if he received mail from them with information about the Main Street Project, chatting fast, trying to keep the black thoughts out of my mind.

He surprised me with his answers. He was informed, and, without a doubt, he had all his marbles.

"I'd like to ask you some questions about Sheila Balfour, if you don't mind."

I didn't know what his reaction to that would be. If he moved to get the shotgun, would I still have a chance to get out the door first? And, if I did get out, would I be able to make it to my car in time?

No.

But he set his mug down and stared at it. Then he looked up at me. His light green eyes held tears as he bent his head facing the Formica top again. "'Scuse me." He got up and went to the back of the trailer. My heart tripped loudly. Was he getting another gun?

He came back with a large framed picture. The girl in the picture smiled, and for a second I felt slightly dizzy. The face could have been Missy's, Loren's daughter, but the hair style in the high school graduation picture was of another generation.

I read the inscription. "To my most favorite person in the whole world, Sheila."

Sheila, Loren's sister and Missy's aunt.

Charlie smiled back at the picture. "She keeps me company all the time. I talk to her and I hear her talking back. I keep looking at her, so pretty, but what I see in the mirror is some old goat. What happened? I don't feel that I changed. How did I get so old?"

The skin was taut on his face. The only wrinkles were around his eyes, but I thought they came from squinting in the desert sunlight, not from laughing. He didn't look like he laughed much.

"So pretty, happy all the time." He fondled the frame, lost in the memory of her eyes.

"Tell me about her." I wanted to hear his version.

"We wanted to get married. In those days, we needed the family's approval. Neither one of us had any money, but that didn't bother me. I was eighteen; I could get a job anywhere. I'm a really good mechanic. At least I was back then. We didn't care where we lived. Here, in this trailer. She would have liked it. Open spaces. She didn't like a lot of people around, neither did I. Just the two of us. Sort of like it is now. Only..." he trailed off, and looked into the picture.

"Yes?" I said, trying to encourage him to go on, as though my energy would draw the story out of him.

"Everything was fine when we were in high school. We saw each other all the time, were in the school play, did everything together, but when we graduated we had to find ways to see each other. Sheila's father was a real tyrant. He practically kept her a prisoner. If she went anywhere, somebody had to be with her. It was usually Loren."

He sipped his coffee, still gazing at the picture.

"Loren didn't like playing watchdog anymore than Sheila liked having him around. But Loren did everything Poppa told him to do. Of course we met and had wonderful times. We were in love, and we had to be together all the time. Then one day, we were having sodas at the Pine Coffee Shop. And the old man came by and saw us. He marched in and grabbed her by the hair, trying to pull her out of there, screaming about her being the whore of

Babylon."

He paused, looking down at the table again. I could see the pulse in his neck throbbing rapidly. "Seems like yesterday. I can still hear him. He went crazy. Couldn't understand it. What did we do?" he appealed to me.

I shook my head.

"I grabbed him, he punched me in the mouth, and Sheila pounded on him. He finally dragged her out. And then I heard he took a whip to her. I thought about killing..."

He paused, and swallowed.

"The old man wouldn't let me see her at all after that. I found out later he told her all sorts of terrible things. That I embezzled money from the store and married some floozy. All lies. Lies to make her give me up. I tried to see her, even went there at night to knock on her window. Would you believe the old coot had the window to her room boarded up?"

I thought about how it must have been for him, how I would feel.

He stood up. I hoped he wasn't relating me in any way to his anger against old Mr. Balfour. He moved away from the table. I kept an eye on the shotgun at the door. He poured coffee into his cup. My cup was still full. I began to sip. I didn't want him to get mad because he thought I didn't like his coffee.

"He even went so far as to have a newspaper printed up about me getting married and showed it to her. That did it."

He stood for a moment. His head almost reached the ceiling of the trailer.

"After that, she lost her mind. She used to get out of the house in the middle of the night and wander around town like a bag lady." Charlie snorted. "It sure got back at the old man. Couldn't do a thing about it. He gave up locking her in her room, figured she wasn't worth anything to anyone anyhow. That I wouldn't want her anymore. I tried to bring her out of it, but it was no use. My Sheila was gone. Couldn't stand it anymore. So I left town, came out here, got into the construction business, and tried to live like a hermit." He let out a huge sigh that sounded like it came all the way up from under the trailer.

"Have you kept up with all of the other things that have been happening to the family?"

"Old man died. Knew that. Serves him right for all he did." Charlie looked like he was getting angry again, cords showing in his neck and his color bright pink. He got up quickly, grabbed the coffee pot and poured some into my cup, dripping across the table. He ripped off a paper towel and dabbed at the drops. A little faster and harder than necessary.

I realized I had a vice grip on my cup. I wanted to calm him down. How to do that? I was mesmerized by his story, transported back to those years.

"Knew Sheila tried to commit suicide. Guess that's when Loren finally decided to put her in an asylum. He had those three young'uns, and she was still living with them in the family house. I will give him credit for trying to make it up to her after the old man went. Treated her like royalty. Too late then. He should've stood up to the old man in the first place."

"How did Mr. Balfour die?" I didn't know why I even asked him that question. I could have found the information out easily, and elsewhere. Sometimes I'm psychic. This seemed to be one of those times for the question had a startling affect on Charlie, considering he had brought the subject up.

"Just a car crash, is all. People have them all the time. Think you should leave. I don't want to talk about those times anymore." His shotgun voice was back. "Don't want you coming back here anymore. That's the past. It's dead. Everybody's dead."

"Charlie—"

"Get out."

I raised my hands palms up in a gesture of surrender, and slid out of the booth. He opened the screen door for me. I looked down at the shotgun by the door, and felt my stomach lurch. The holes of it seemed to be shooting out red flames. I held onto the door frame for a moment, dizzy.

"Get out," he said softly, holding Sheila's picture in his other hand.

Back on the road, I pulled off when I was in sight of the freeway on ramp and a long way from Charlie and his shotgun. I wrote down everything that I could remember from the conversation and made a list of questions to which I wanted answers. Including how old Mr. Balfour died. Now I was curious.

Charlie may have wanted to see Loren out of the picture years ago, but was that still true? Why would he want him dead? Selling his property in Mirasol didn't seem to be high on Charlie's agenda. If it had been, he would have attended the Coalition of Ten meetings or communicated with them more.

He'd have to drive into Mirasol for those meetings, but going back to the town didn't seem to be something he ever wanted to do.

I closed the notebook and drove onto the freeway, my mind speeding faster than the car.

Chapter 19
Saturday Evening

Two and a half hours and a million thoughts later, I pulled into my driveway, then pressed the garage door opener. Paul, my next door neighbor, called over the fence.

"Dawn's in the hospital."

His wife. Due to have a baby. I wanted to ask about it but the look on Paul's face hinted at tragedy.

I turned the engine off and looked over at him.

"What happened?" I said.

"Wheel came off while she was driving. She lost control and ran into a couple of parked cars."

"Is she okay?" I asked.

"We almost lost the baby."

"Oh, no!" It was their first. They were really excited, even had a party as soon as she knew for sure she was pregnant. The baby would be one lucky person to be born to this couple. The baby had to be okay.

"Somebody did it on purpose," he said.

"Why do you say that?"

"Police said the lug nuts were loose. Would have blamed it on the place where we get our car serviced, but I just changed that tire. No way were those lug nuts loose. Used my brother-in-law's tools. I wanted to tell you, warn you, in case somebody might tamper with yours."

My body went cold.

"You two both drive the same red convertibles. We had ours in the carport as usual, so anyone can see it from the street. Probably just kids, but you'd better keep yours in the garage locked up. I wouldn't leave it out for anybody to get at." His voice was high-pitched, anxious.

Could he possibly be right? Why would anyone want to fool with my car?

"Thanks, Paul. So you told the police that somebody tampered with it?"

"Sure did. First thing out of my mouth when the cop said something about the lug nuts. Nobody else's car got bothered. Lots of carports on this street. So thought maybe it was the car. Maybe the red attracted them. You'd think they'd want to steal it, not mess with it."

He shook his head. "Going back to the hospital now. Just wanted to warn you." Paul moved away as though he couldn't bear to talk about it anymore.

"Let me know if I can do anything," I called after him, feeling ineffectual. I couldn't think of anything better to say than that triteness. He waved acknowledgement, not turning back, his head bent. I thought he must be crying.

Dawn and I had bought identical cars almost the same day. We'd done a double take over our backyard fence at each other's cars.

"People told me not to buy a red car," she had said. "They said I'm more likely to get a ticket. I told them I've always had a red car, and when I drove fast I got a ticket, and when I didn't, I didn't—red car or not." And then she had laughed, a beautiful musical sound. She was about five feet tall with, dark curly hair, blue, blue eyes, and at the time becoming plump with child.

I squeezed my eyes in frustration.

Who would do that to someone's car? Were they trying to hurt the person who drove the car? Who would want to hurt Dawn?

What if they had made a mistake in the cars?

What if they were really after my car?

How long would the loose lug nuts have held while I traveled on the freeway to Palm Springs today? I thought I'd done well to escape Charlie's shotgun, thought I was safe when I was in my car going at a high rate of speed toward home.

I wouldn't be in the hospital.

I wouldn't have ended up in anything as pleasant as a hospital.

Chapter 20
Sunday Noon

Shopping for groceries Sunday noon was not a good idea. Everyone was there in their Sunday-go-to-meeting outfits looking askance at those of us casually dressed as though we had a scarlet A on our breasts.

I'd hope to cut down on the stress of the crowds by going to a new upscale market, Leicester Farms. Pronounced 'Lester,' if you please, the ads said. Couldn't help thinking about Lester Barrone at the law firm. Wondered if the store sold wild bowties.

A coffee bar adjoined the bakery. Mary Cordero sat at a table and waved me over just as the woman seated beside her rose and went to the counter. Recognition of the woman took a moment, my mental computer clanking, as I hadn't seen her since our high school days. What the heck was her name? I made my way to their table.

"My baby daughter," Mary said looking after her with pride in her eyes, "a travel agent in Arcadia. Our kids are getting us a trip to Hawaii for our forty-fifth wedding anniversary."

"Mary, that's wonderful on both counts—Hawaii and a forty-fifth." I was envious because I knew I'd never have one of the latter.

Nicole. That was her name. It came to me as I watched her weave her way back with coffee and pastries.

The area was small, gradually filling with more people wandering in and eyeing those who looked like they might be finishing up their delectable treats.

She had a paper plate of cannoli, éclair, cream puff, and a fruit tart. All the food groups, including chocolate.

We chatted about Hawaii and where Nicole had booked them. Both of them telling me the details, both excited, Mary because she was going, and Nicole because she was giving her mother something wonderful. For a few moments I was transported there, my current bare refrigerator and cupboard forgotten.

Nicole made an 'mmmm' sound as she bit into what looked like a two-million- calorie cream-filled chocolate éclair.

"We went there a few times with the Balfours and the Hawkins years ago when the kids were little," Mary said. "Always love to go back. But without the kids." She gave Nicole a big grin and squeezed her hand.

"Oh, you reminded me of something odd," Nicole said, wiping a flake of chocolate from her upper lip. "Loren Balfour coming to my office. Thought he came because he knew who my Mom was." She returned a pride-filled look to Mary. "I was really pleased, but then I realized he didn't know me from Eve. Didn't recognize me at all. I never said anything about it."

Mary looked a little puzzled. I wasn't getting a good feeling.

"Loren bought cruise tickets to Hawaii."

But that wasn't the odd part that Nicole wanted to tell us, I was sure.

"Two one-way tickets."

For a second, I thought she got the numbers mixed up. "One way? As in 'no return'?"

She nodded. "Made out to Mr. and Mrs. Loren Balfour."

"One way, and then flying back?" said Mary.

"No," she said as she wiped chocolate off her fingers. "The way he talked, he sounded like he wasn't ever coming back. He didn't make any return flight reservations. I thought that was odd."

I played that line through my mental computer. "When were the tickets for?" My voice croaked out the words. But I knew.

"That's even odder. Last Sunday they were going to leave," she said. "The Sunday he killed himself."

Chapter 21
Monday A.M.

Back in my office, I sat in my chair and thought about the cruise tickets some more. I wanted to talk to Win Balfour again. See what she knew about the tickets. I had the feeling she wouldn't know anything. Maybe it was a surprise for their wedding anniversary like Mary and Corky's children were doing for them, I thought optimistically. But all I could think about was the Sunday morning lady friend. And the figurine of the boy and girl in Hawaiian outfits.

Maybe Cal and I were wrong. Maybe it had been for Win. I had to find out for sure about the figurine. Had Loren been planning to tuck the cruise tickets under the maraschino cherry bow of the gift and give it to Win?

No, the timing was off. He wouldn't give her the tickets the day they were sailing.

The paperwork on my large desk had spawned itself several times over. I was there looking at it by 7:30. Audrey usually came in at eight. Almost on the dot, she opened the connecting door. In her hand was a steaming pot of coffee, and on her face, a big smile. "We must have had a very nice weekend in Palm Springs."

"I didn't stay there but it was an okay weekend." No bad dreams. In fact, I had even sailed to Hawaii a couple of times. Why did she ask that? Did I look rested? Or the opposite, as though I'd stayed up the whole time partying? Maybe it was just because I was smiling, something I hadn't done a lot of lately.

"Apparently." She grinned when she started to pour coffee into my cup. I grabbed the cup and took a look. No dead fly.

"Hey, thanks," I said. She must have washed it.

"Thank you," Audrey said.

"You must have had a good weekend." Her grin had to be for

something.

"No complaints," she said as she walked out and closed the door, still grinning. And here I thought her career Navy boyfriend was out on a long cruise.

Since she was in such a good mood, she wouldn't mind a few extra things on her pile. I wrote instructions on the pleadings, letters, memos, and made up a 'to do' list for both of us.

I set her share on her desk as she held the phone to her ear and typed on the computer keyboard. I pointed downstairs to the police department. She nodded.

Downstairs, I snagged the busy desk officer and asked her who had replaced Cal.

Garbage Mouth was in Oregon picking up a prisoner. Mr. Personality was on vacation. Unfortunately for him, his vacation was at home in Mirasol painting his house. Therefore reachable.

One whiff of the frenzied air in P. D. convinced me not to stay. I didn't want to be the first person in line to talk with Mr. Personality. At least I knew who was on the duty roster.

Quon Lee was on my 'to do' list. I wanted a description of the Sunday morning lady friend to compare with the one I had from the lady on Cremona. Seemed likely there'd be a match. At least I knew for sure she really existed. I wanted Quon Lee to tell me who she was. And I wanted to know more about his lawsuit against Loren, but that could wait. I'd have to play the question game. Okay, I could do that.

Next on my list was Mary Cordero, to ask her about old Mr. Balfour's death in the car accident all those years ago. Why had my question about the death upset Charlie?

Next item was to return to the house on Nutwood across the street from the church. Its side faced the back of Quon Lee's diner and the alley. I still wanted to know if anyone there saw the Sunday morning lady friend. And if they saw her every Sunday. Also, who did they see last Sunday?

I checked my watch. A good time for a cup of apple blossoms.

When he gave me coffee, he started talking. No game playing today, it seemed. I was getting my questions, which I hadn't even asked yet, answered.

"Like he only one with somethin' to lose," Quon Lee said from behind the counter where four headless, plucked chickens lay. "He never generous when business on table."

I had come in the side door so I stood with Quon Lee behind the counter watching him do unmentionable things to those chickens.

Whack.

Another piece came off. Suddenly, I had no desire for the coffee Quon Lee poured for me. I had a terrible taste in my mouth. I set the cup and saucer down, the dark liquid sloshing against a pink petal.

Whack.

"Old man and I agree. My customers use his parking lot. Driveway too. Now all potholes. Big enough for car to fall down."

Quon Lee almost didn't exaggerate. The driveway was full of potholes, deep ones.

"Loren come here one day. Cry." He pantomimed tears running down his cheeks, blood dripping from the cleaver he held. "I give him cuppa coffee. Good." He gestured with the bloody cleaver toward my cup. "Business bad, he say. What he expect? Old stuff in store. Who buy? Old ladies, but old ladies die. Nobody go in. What he thinks? I tell him."

Whack.

Now all the legs were off. I felt nauseous and cold.

"Then he cries some more. He say sons want sell to city. Get new store. Wah, wah, he cry. I listen. We know each other long time." Quon Lee was telling me more than I'd ever be able to ask for.

"He only come here when he get bad news. His place falling down. He never do anything. Plumbing, electric, roof leak. Everything. He say city must fix everything. Make store like new. He not to use his money. Never to use his money."

Whack.

Wings off.

"City say they tear down, build new, not fix up." Quon Lee waved the still-dripping cleaver toward the other end of the street.

"His face red. Like this." He pointed to the chicken blood. "He too upset for regular person about keeping store. I say mid-life crisis."

I wanted to ask Quon Lee what he knew about a mid-life crisis. That would back up everyone's theory about suicide. But I let Quon Lee talk. No game playing today. What had set him off? At the moment, I didn't care because I was feeling so queasy.

"He say nobuddy tear store down. He say he lay front of bulldozer. He say that." Almost the same thing Skip had told me.

Quon Lee separated the chicken pieces. Even though the door and customer window were open, I couldn't breathe. Nothing seemed more important than getting out into the air. I nodded and gave a slight wave goodbye.

The last thing I heard was another Whack.

I left.

My stomach felt like I had swallowed a block of grease. Audrey's coffee. I had only taken a few sips and could still taste it. My stomach was doing strange things.

And I was staggering. What would anyone think? Particularly if they knew who I was?

The Corderos lived just two streets away. I passed Cremona and my sweet, pink-shawled, chocolate chip cookie maker. Things gurgled in the area of my upper diaphragm. Cookies didn't sound at all tempting.

The Cordero house was in sight. I felt like a traveler in the desert, crawling on my hands and knees. October in Southern California and the temperature close to 80.

"Funny that all the buildings the city council people own are in the part of town that's doing good. If we had just one of them owning a building in our section, I bet things would happen fast." Mary Cordero was stretched out on a lounge chair on their concrete patio, a glass of homemade lemonade in hand. She shook the glass every time before she drank so that the ice cubes rattled and a sweetish smell of the drink came to me. Not pleasant.

Nothing small about their backyard, nor the profundity of the flowers. Almost like being in Hawaii. Rich and bright colors in wild abandon bordered the green lawn, carefully cut as though one blade at a time. The scene was wavering before my eyes. No, my eyes were wavering. What was wrong?

Stretched out on the other lounge chair, I didn't want to move for fear the nausea would start again. I was sleepy, drifting in and out, hearing some of Mary's words. Maybe I had the flu.

"I've lived in this town a long time and seen a lot of things. I remember Loren shaking his fist at us. 'I'll never sell, never,' he said. Maybe suicide was his way out."

For some reason I was feeling both sleepy and nauseated. I tried to concentrate on her words. She thought he might have done it?

"But he did have a point, said the city tried to take him to the cleaners big time. Trying to take his store, and paying him nothing for it. After all it's still open and doing a good business."

Part of what she was saying didn't compute with what Skip had told me.

"I gotta tell you, the price the city offered us was okay. Not great, but okay. Considering we can't sell the darn thing anyway, I shouldn't complain."

She turned to me. "Loren's store is doing well. Making a lot of money, he says. So the price should be higher, right? But it wasn't." Mary Cordero shook her head. I made a mental note to ask Skip about the money. Quon Lee didn't seem to think that the store flourished. That didn't jibe with what he said Loren had told him. Wishful thinking on Quon Lee's part? Or Loren just bragging to Mary? Who was right?

"Why was the city squeezing him on one hand," Mary Cordero said, "and then complaining that he wasn't cooperating on the other? I think if they offered him a fair price he might have sold it."

I nodded, trying to stay awake. I wanted to sit up, try to keep alert. I seemed to be slipping down on the lounge chair. Whenever I moved, my stomach gave another painful lurch.

"What are you going to do when you sell?" I asked, saying something just to move me out of my lethargy.

Mary Cordero rotated her wrist with her words, "A little of this, a little of that. Visit some golf courses. Corky loves to golf. God knows why. I only like riding around on the golf cart. Those courses in Hawaii, you should see them. Like I've died and gone to heaven."

It kept coming back to Hawaii. Had to see Win. Soon.

Beautiful as the scene was I had to get out of there and go

home. To bed. At the moment the two choices were whether I wanted more to go to sleep or to throw up.

"Corky and me really don't have any plans. We're not going to run off to Palm Springs and buy a big condo or a few acres in Oregon or anything like that. Why does everybody have to move when they retire? Hey, I like this town. Too late to be starting over again. Trying to find a new gas station, a new dry cleaners. Happy with what I've got now. Couldn't meet any nicer people than the ones that live in this town. Suits me just fine."

Now or never. "Mary, would it be too much to ask you to drive me home? I'm not feeling well." Actually, I'm dying, I wanted to say.

"Let's go," she said, sliding off the chaise lounge.

Chapter 22
Monday to Tuesday

I was too sick to call Dr. Del. Everything came up from as far down as my toenails. Several times.

Dreams. Delirium. Nate and I were back on the case. Sonnyboy kept firing, then grabbing another shotgun and doing it all over. Over and over. He'd shot me in the stomach—I could feel the pain.

Waking up at eight on Tuesday morning, I didn't feel great, but I also didn't think I'd feel better if I was dead.

In the kitchen, I was surprised to find the numeral four blinking on my answering machine. I hadn't heard the phone ring. Not that I would have cared. And I didn't have any idea where I had set the phone down last. Had to be when I left for work yesterday.

All from City Hall's information desk trying to locate me. I'd see the clerk when I made it to the office.

I got ready, put makeup on the would-be corpse, and drove instead of walking to work. The one-mile hike was beyond the realm of my physique at the moment. Let alone my plan to run every morning. I heard myself groan at the thought.

Weak and shaking, I decided some tomato juice might help. That hadn't been part of my refrigerator's inventory at home. Coaxing three small cans out of the old vending machine at City Hall, I drank them as though I was dying of thirst. I had almost died of something.

Forget the one flight of stairs. I took the elevator. The swaying movement brought the nausea back.

Audrey's coffee cup on her desk. Coffeepot half full. I gagged. At first I thought she'd just stepped out for a minute. But there was a ghostlike aura about our offices. No smell of just-brewed coffee.

I touched the cup. Cold. Ditto for the pot.

Silence and coldness. No smell of a human presence.

Yesterday's coffee.

Where was Audrey?

A call to the information desk elicited a gush of relief from the woman who answered.

"I've been trying to reach you. I didn't want to leave a message other than to call me."

Audrey was in the hospital. Yesterday morning. Paramedics. Mirasol General. Dr. Delbert.

A call to him.

Audrey in critical condition.

Poisoned.

I told him my bout with what I thought was the flu. He told me what to do. Part of which was bed rest and plenty of fluids. I could do the latter. I looked at the level of the coffee pot. She'd had at least two cups; I'd only had a couple of swallows. I told him that also.

Down to P.D. on the elevator again to report the possible poisoning of Audrey and me. An accident of some sort? It certainly gave a new meaning to the term 'bad coffee.' Maybe I was just being dramatic when I told them we were poisoned deliberately.

They sent an officer up to collect the evidence and deliver a sample to Dr. Del so he could figure out what kind of poison it was. It would help him to better treat Audrey.

I felt claustrophobic as though the coffee poison permeated the air and I breathed it. I wanted to find out who and why.

Musing, I walked back and forth in front of the windows looking over the palm trees to the mountains. Still clear today. I could see the mountains, but they were backed up against a dull brown sky. Smog.

Why were we poisoned? Who? Disgruntled citizen? Why the city attorney's office? It wasn't exactly the easiest place to find in City Hall.

Pacing some more. Outside, a breeze fluttered the palm fronds. City attorney the target? Or Audrey? Or me? Me. But why? The sun through the windows felt warm. Loved to drive up Lake Street into Altadena. I could almost hug the mountains, they were that close.

My hands were like ice. Like the snow in December on the

mountains farther off. That was an awesome sight.

Yesterday morning replayed in my head, overlaying the view of the mountains. Then it dawned on me. Audrey hadn't made the coffee. She arrived after I did. I remembered our conversation. She thought I had made the coffee. That's what she meant about having a good weekend in Palm Springs. She must have thought it was so good that I had bounded out of bed on Monday morning, came to work and made coffee for her.

Someone else had made the coffee. And put something in it.

I stopped at the end of the windows. My hands were so cold that my fingers were numb.

Too many variables, too many thoughts were elbowing each other in my mind.

The phone rang.

Then I realized I didn't have Audrey to answer it. I knew the operator would get it after five rings. I picked it up.

Florence Hedden, manager of the Banquet Hall Restaurant, announced herself. She wanted to remind Audrey about their appointment to select the colors for the linens at the commissioners' dinner. I hazily recalled Audrey talking about it, something she planned every year.

The normality of it, something from a non-sordid world where birds sang in the trees, kids played on the street, and mothers loved their children. No death, poison, or anything sinister. A reason to get out of the office.

"I'll be right over, Florence."

"...the tablecloths," said Florence.

I bathed in the gentleness of Florence's world at the Banquet Hall Restaurant. Audrey had ordered a gourmet Italian dinner. Everything so normal.

I stood looking at the linens, the ghost of a memory wavering into shape. It shimmered in my mind and then the pattern came into focus.

"That's it!"

"Oh, you want the red with white napkins?" she waved the napkin open across the table.

"No, no," I said.

"Then the white with red—" but I looked right through her seeing that night of the chamber mixer. That was it! The door prizes. A checked tablecloth. Not polka dots. Checks. Red and white. Donated by a trattoria. And it had been won.

The scene was clear in my mind. The shy winner went up to receive it, murmuring thanks into the microphone thrust at her.

Marti.

Marti holding up the opened tablecloth. It practically covered her whole body. She must have been showing it to Loren in the parking lot. And he kissed her. That's what Dottie had seen. The checkered tablecloth. Not polka dots.

"You pick it, Florence. I've got to go to the hospital to see a sick friend."

"Maybe green then—"

That was all I heard as I headed for the door.

"We were meeting."

"That Sunday, you mean?" I said.

"Yes, but...that day was different. Late...couldn't find my keys for the car...and then I saw..." The tears were flooding in her eyes. Marti's blonde hair lay tangled on the pillow.

"You met Loren every Sunday?"

Marti nodded.

I'd found Loren's Sunday morning lady friend. I'd get Quon Lee to confirm it without impinging on his sense of gentlemanliness, and the lady on Cremona would have to ID her also.

She talked slowly. She seemed weak and slightly sedated. Her mouth moved unnaturally, as though one side had a shot of something from the dentist. I looked at the bottle feeding into her arm. I felt like I was trying to illicit a deathbed confession. She wasn't dying, but maybe she wanted to, maybe she was trying to.

"I parked across the street in the church lot. Then I went to the store. Loren always left the door unlocked and turned on a light for me." Her voice was now a whisper.

"What happened that Sunday?" I said.

Dust in her throat from her long silence about Loren. Marti coughed and tried to reach for the water. I gave her the plastic glass with the bent straw.

"So late. My keys. I couldn't find them. I shouldn't have spent so much time looking for them. I should have just started walking right away, but so much to think about..." She became agitated, running out of breath as though she was still looking for the keys and not finding them.

"I called him, but there was no answer. Finally I walked, ran. He'd be wondering if I was coming, if I had changed my mind." She took a breath, more of a gasp. "When I got there all the lights were on..." her eyes closed, "the ambulance...."

I could see her chest vibrating rapidly. If I was a responsible citizen, I would ring for the nurse. Instead, I waited, wanting to hear what she would say. Maybe this was the therapy she needed.

"...went across the street to church...so frightened. All our plans..." She weakly waved her hand. "I guess I went to pray. I couldn't imagine what had happened. Maybe a heart attack. But not...what happened."

The tears were sliding out of the corners of her eyes and onto the pillow. Onto her hair.

Neither of us noticed Kirby until he walked through the door.

"Why, Jo, how nice of you to visit Marti." I stood up as he pumped my hand. I looked into his eyes trying to determine if he had heard anything or knew what we were talking about, but I couldn't tell.

I made my goodbyes. What to say to her? Even if I found the right word I couldn't talk in front of Kirby. But Marti didn't look as though she cared about much. I mumbled something about being on my way to see Mother.

Then I headed for Mother's room. I'd kill a little time until I could see Marti again—alone. I still had questions to ask her. I wanted to be sure Kirby left the hospital before I talked with her again. I shoved any guilt pangs at badgering an ill person to a box in my mind and clamped the lid down. As I had on other thoughts. I didn't want to think.

Mother was about to be sprung, or so she believed. "Delbert says maybe tomorrow." 'Maybe' didn't seem very positive to me, but I knew she could handle Dr. Del. She looked ready to walk out on her crutches. "You must feed my violets. This is their regular day." Feed them? I hadn't even watered the little rascals. "The eyedropper is in—"

Eyedropper!

Then more specific instructions as to how to mix the food. "You will do that, won't you, sweetie?"

I agreed, yes, I would go to her house to feed her plants as soon as I left the hospital. Next I'd be changing their diapers.

If I wanted to, I could spend the whole afternoon at Mirasol General. I thought I should visit Dawn and learn whether her baby was going to be all right.

I only spent most of the afternoon at Mirasol General.

Kirby was with Marti when I walked by, so I just waved to them.

Dawn was sound asleep when I peeked in, which relieved me of trying to think of something meaningful to say. I decided to leave the hospital, not wanting to try to visit Marti again in case I ran into Kirby.

But thinking of Marti made me think of Win, Loren's widow. Director of Volunteers. She was definitely on my "to do" list. What about the one-way tickets to Hawaii?

I asked the first white-coated person I saw how to get to her office. The ground floor, make a right at the water fountain—I remembered about as much of the directions as Mother had told me about mixing the plant food.

The ground floor was a labyrinth.

Eventually, with enough people directing, I found her.

I stepped in, closed the door, and sat down on a chair in front of her desk. On the chair next to me sat a giant Teddy Bear. At least, that's what his nameplate said.

I had caught Win still in her office.

She wore a bright turquoise tailored suit, which set off her well-styled short white hair. When she saw me, she stared for a moment, nodded, and laid her pen down. As though she had expected me. As though, like Marti and Quon Lee, she had been waiting for the right person to come along to hear her story.

Where to start? What did she know about Loren's plans? I merely told her I was wrapping up the files on her husband's death and wanted to ask her a few questions. But that's as far as I got, for she grabbed the ball and ran with it, moving into the past.

"It all started in Hawaii," she said as though she was continuing a phantom conversation with me. "Eight of us rented a house together. October. Three years ago this month. Loren and Marti sat out on the lanai. For hours. The whole two weeks. Just talking. Sometimes they went for a walk along the beach, but never out of sight of the house. Observing the proprieties of behavior."

Another possibility was that they were afraid to be alone together when they were in Hawaii.

Win took a gold case out of her purse and snapped it open. It looked as though it held business cards, but instead I saw five cigarettes inside. "I'm not supposed to smoke here, but..." She left the sentence for Teddy and me to finish. She flipped open the top of a gold lighter and lit the cigarette. I could almost feel her pleasure when she pulled the smoke in. I wanted to hold my breath. The room was small. With Teddy there, it was over the occupancy limit.

"At first I was mad with jealousy. Loren, alive, full of energy, laughing, acting like he was 17 years old again. That's how old he was when we met in high school. He hadn't been like that with me for years. In fact, he'd almost turned into an old man. I was glad I had this job. It saved my sanity. I had to get out of the house every day, meet with other people. Otherwise I don't know what I would have done."

Another draw on the cigarette. A long one. She blew the smoke upward. The stream hit the low ceiling, and seemed to bounce on an angle right toward me.

"One day really stands out in my mind. That day on the lanai when they were talking and laughing. He seemed so happy. His eyes were shining, like a kid at Christmas. I'm glad of it now. At least he had that. But back then I was livid when the realization hit me."

"Realization of what?" I asked.

"What being happy meant. I hadn't been happy for years. All that wasted time. Both of us. Going through the motions of life. Not really getting any joy out of anything. At least I wasn't. Trying to find some meaning in our lives by getting involved in the community. Keep busy and you'll forget you're not happy. Not happily married. What I realized that day was I hadn't known I wasn't happy. I didn't know there could be a life for me outside of what I was doing." She stopped talking for a moment and looked at her hands.

"I realized it all when I saw how happy Loren was. Your generation is different. That's good. My generation, some of us, lived a life of quiet desperation. Oh, that sounds like such a cliché. But it's one they can put on my tombstone." She laughed with no merriment.

She tugged at a tissue from the box on a shelf behind her. She touched her eyes with it. "I finally made the decision to talk to Loren about a divorce. File even if he wouldn't agree. To hell with him, I thought." She pulled on the cigarette again. The tiny room now filled with smoke.

"Then he killed himself. I thought somehow he sensed I was going to tell him that we should get divorced. That we couldn't go on. I thought that's why he...why he did it." She looked at Teddy for judgment.

I sensed her tension, her relief at confessing. She still sat like a ramrod in her chair, looking over Teddy's head, cigarette expiring.

I wanted to tell her that I felt guilty, too, and why. And that maybe Loren didn't kill himself. Would that offer her any comfort, any hope? Somehow it seemed better just to let her talk.

"I was so mad at Loren for escaping like that. Leaving me without any explanation or resolution. Like he was too disgusted with everything to even try to keep up pretenses any longer."

Suddenly a knock on the door made us both jump. She quickly pushed at the lighted end trying to kill all the embers. And then she shoved the ashtray into a side drawer. She went to the door.

The hospital smell gusted up my nostrils, pushing away the dead smoke.

Maybe Mother was right about the Chanel No. 5.

A minor emergency with a volunteer staff member. She had to go.

"One question, Win. Did you have a trip planned to Hawaii?'

"No." She looked startled that I even asked the question. "To tell you the truth, I don't ever want to go back there. Ever."

"You weren't planning a vacation there about this time?"

"I've got a major training workshop for the volunteers coming up. There's no way I'd be taking a vacation now."

"And Loren knew that?"

"It's the same time every year. It's on the calendar in the kitchen. Got to go."

And she did.

Definitely not Win who was going to play Mrs. Loren Balfour on the trip to Hawaii.

Chapter 23
Wednesday A.M.

I had found the phone last night buried under newspapers on the floor in the living room. I couldn't remember putting either the newspapers or the phone there. Then I noticed the ringer was on the lowest volume setting. Had I done that, too? I usually kept it on my nightstand. My memory was so foggy.

Yesterday, when I made my report at the police department, they didn't seem overly enthusiastic about my suggestion that someone had poisoned Audrey and me. Hard for me to believe, so how could I expect them to be hot to investigate my accusation?

I checked in with them in the morning to finish answering any questions they had regarding my statement. Now they, a woman and a man, both sworn personnel, hoped I would go away. A poisoning in City Hall one floor up from their office wasn't good for their image, said the vibes I was getting.

They asked if Audrey and I had lunch together. Maybe we got food poisoning someplace. A statement on their part.

"Who made it to lunch?" I asked them. "I was sick before that."

"How about breakfast?" they asked.

"I don't eat breakfast." Except on the weekends. But I didn't think they needed the details of my interesting social life. We went round a few more times, they hoping to find a possibility other than the one I and Audrey, in absentia, presented.

They drank coffee furiously, and offered me a cup. I told them I'd given it up, it seemed healthier. They thought that funny.

While they were laughing, I focused on a small red ribbon pinned to the collar of the white blouse worn by the police sergeant who took the report.

Red. Maraschino red bow. The Hawaii figurines.

While they were still laughing, I asked to check a package out of property. That was another person, and more paperwork, but I got the figurine Cal had showed me.

I took it up to my office. A strange woman sat at Audrey's desk. Fifty-ish, short brown hair. Friendly, pretty face and a little-girl voice. When she stood to shake hands, I almost had to look up at her. She had to be at least six feet tall. Good grip. We introduced ourselves. Kathryn. Loved her smile. Handpicked by Deb. One of a senior partner's two secretaries. Well, well, well.

She seemed impressed that I commanded such attention from the firm. Me, too, I wanted to tell her. And I was curious. They weren't getting any more complaints from the city, at least none that I knew about, so why not keep me happy? Then I wouldn't go back to Lester A. Barrone. Little did they know I wasn't going back anyhow.

But now they had a poisoning case on their hands. What did they think about that?

I immediately assessed that Kathryn knew her job, a veteran of the firm. I left her to the paperwork, thanking the gods for looking after me—sometimes.

I took the figurine out of the box and set it on the big conference table desk. Talk to me, you two, you with the lei and you with the ukulele.

The gift puzzled me. If Loren was going to give it to Marti as a present, why did he kill himself before she got there? Did he think she wasn't coming and he couldn't bear life without her?

What if the gift was for someone else? But for whom? Not Win. That would be too much like malice, and I didn't see Loren in the role.

What about Eric? He got there just after Marti's usual arrival time, but his father was already dead. Dead after the time Marti should have been there. That fact bothered me.

I leaned back in my chair, looking over the palm trees and the north part of Mirasol to the mountains, now hidden behind a smog haze. I let my mind free float. Maybe I had liked being a criminal lawyer so much because I loved puzzles. I had no desire to go back to it, but I had a puzzle on my hands right now. I couldn't say I was enjoying it because it was Loren's death, but it felt familiar, and I felt confident in my ability to fit all the pieces together. If it was murder.

The feelings I got were mixed. The time element was out of kilter. The lady with the pink shawl had a time line of people coming and going from the store, and that time line differed from the one I had. The only fact I could rely on was when the call came in, Eric calling 911, and the time the paramedics arrived at 9:30.

I looked over the light brown haze to the foothills. And thought about hiking along the trail, seeing the waterfalls and smelling the cool, fresh air full of the scent of real pine trees and the wildflowers in the canyons. Where I wished I was. Even if I was, I'd probably still be contemplating this puzzle.

I was still considering that it was possible Loren did commit suicide in a sudden fit of depression, trying to fit in the facts I had with that scenario. I had to think like a lawyer.

My "to do" list:

A visit to Marti.

And Audrey.

Visiting Mother and Dawn flitted through my mind but I was working, I told myself, not socializing, so they could be left for another time. And Win—no more questions for her at the moment.

When I got back I had to stop by the P.D. to talk with Mr. Personality. I couldn't put it off any longer. I wanted some interviews done and I needed to make up a time schedule as to who was where and when.

I let Kathryn know where I was headed and drove to Mirasol General again, and the hospital smell.

Marti slowly pulled the figurine out of the box and held it up to look at it. She was propped up slightly, but still seemed weak.

I didn't tell her where the figurine was found. I just asked if she'd ever seen it before.

"No. It's so pretty." She looked at it lovingly. Loren had made a good choice in a present.

"What about at Jayne's Gift Shop? Ever seen it there, perhaps?" I wondered if maybe she had, and had mentioned it to Loren.

She shook her head, her honey-blonde hair twisting on the pillow, and the tears were coming faster. "That's what Loren said we were going to do. I would do the hula, and he would play the ukulele."

Ah.

Then I told her where it was found and how it was wrapped up. She still didn't understand.

"Marti, I think it was a gift for you."

She ran her fingers over the boy with the ukulele while the tears dripped from her eyes, but she had a little smile on her face. She held something of Loren's of the moment they were going to have.

"I think he bought it because you are the girl and he is the boy, just as you said."

She nodded, then gulped a few times.

"We were going to Hawaii."

I realized what the "we" meant. I made encouraging noises for her to continue. At least that's what I hoped I sounded like.

"I told him I had to pack a suitcase, but Loren said we could buy whatever we wanted there. Not to bring anything. Leave our old life behind. Everything. Just meet him at the store as..."

"As usual," I said with as much gentleness as I could. "You mean that Sunday? You were going to Hawaii that Sunday?" I thought for a moment. "Forever? As in one way? That Sunday?"

"Yes." Marti came alive, her eyes shone, light refracting through the tears. "Yes," she said softly. I saw the girl face that Loren had seen on the lanai, exploding with happiness. A mirror image of the face of Loren that Win had seen.

"Jo, thank you so much. You don't know what this means to me. We were going to Hawaii, the only place we've ever been happy. We talked about it every Sunday, pretended we were in Hawaii and even drank Kona coffee." She smiled. Beatifically. A saint about to be united with God.

"Marti—" I started to say.

"We were going to live on Molokai."

"Molokai?"

"Loren bought a house there. The island doesn't have a lot of tourists. Kamalo. That's were we were going. On the beach. He showed me the pictures. It's so beautiful."

Molokai to me was reminiscent of my Catholic childhood, Father Damien and the leprosy patients. Didn't sound like a romantic getaway to me.

"The sunset. Oh, have you ever seen the sunset in Hawaii? It's gold...and like peaches. I don't even know the name of the color, but it's so beautiful, orange and pink all mixed together. And the sun just slides into the blue ocean and the sky is all these colors for such a long time and then the trees, the palm trees. That's us," she gestured to the figurine. "That's what we were going to be like."

She took my breath away with her story. "I'm sorry, I truly am," I said. Why did I feel sorrier for Marti than Win? I took her hand. I didn't know what to say.

Marti sobbed, one hand holding the sheet to her face, the figurines toppled over on her lap.

If they were going to Hawaii together that day—

"We—" gulps of sobs stopped her for a moment. "We were going to be picked up at the store. Taken to the ship. Loren got the tickets. All we needed were muumuus and sarongs, and we could get those aboard ship. That's what Loren said. It was going to be so wonderful." She looked into my eyes and almost tore my heart out. "I didn't realize how one person could make me feel so happy," Marti said. She closed her eyes and I watched the tears stream down the sides of her face. I thought about Win. Marti knew the meaning of happiness, but Win didn't. I thought about Ted and wanted to shed tears of my own.

The little boy with a ukulele and the little girl with a lei and grass skirt and flower garland standing next to a palm tree were face down on the white spread as though they, too, had died.

Chapter 24
Wednesday Late Morning

Marti had lost Loren, so why not the figurine too? I told her I would try to get it for her from P.D. when the case was closed. At first she wanted it, then she seemed not to care, as though the effort of seeing it for the first time had drained her. Just as well, because I might not be able to get it back. It belonged to his estate. That meant Win.

When I was at home, my shoes off, I padded around on the cold tile of the kitchen in my stockinged feet. My stomach gurgled, hungry sounds mixed with unwanted juices and poison remnants. Lunch time, but the thought of food just made my stomach burble more. I tried to ignore it. So what was I doing standing here in the kitchen?

One question that wasn't answered to my satisfaction was why Eric was at the store at all on Sunday morning. It seemed to me he didn't normally do that. So why this Sunday? The Sunday his father died. Cal had mentioned something about a phone call at the house. I wondered what that was about. It had been in the police report, also but with no elaboration. I made a note on my 'to do' list.

I hated to admit it, but I wanted to talk to Cal about the case. I was certainly glad to have him out of my hair. But he knew things I didn't, had insights that I didn't. I hated to admit that, too.

I picked up the phone and called Mirasol General. I thought about how my life revolved around that place. Maybe I should put the hospital number into the memory on my telephone. Not my favorite hangout in town, though. A little more coffee that morning and I would have been not a visitor, but a visitee.

This time my call wasn't about a patient. Or to Win.

"Rachel Elkhart, please."

A moment later she picked it up. A miracle.

"Hi, Rachel, it's Jo. I know Cal can only see close relatives, but is there any chance I can get in to talk to him again?"

"Let me work on it," she said. No inflection in her voice either way, yes or no. No asking why. "Call you back."

To forget about the goings on in my stomach, I set sail for the Balfour residence. Win and Eric should both be working. Which meant maybe Missy was there. Alone. I thought it might be nice to see what she had to say.

Missy opened the door, and for a second my heart gave a lurch as it had when I saw the picture of Sheila in Charlie Quinn's hands. Sheila, her aunt.

But I was sure Sheila never wore a bikini. I tried not to look at the low cut top struggling bravely to cover the brown aureoles of her plump breasts.

"Hi, Missy. Is your Mom or Eric here?"

She shook her head and told me where she thought they would be. Oh darn. Since I'm here...

"Can I ask you a few questions?"

Missy held the screen door open for me. She seemed glad of some companionship. "I'm on my way out to the pool. Want something to drink?"

"Sure."

"Gin and tonic?"

Heck, why not? "Sounds great," I said. It must be time for cocktails somewhere in the world. Not likely it could make my stomach any worse. Hopefully, it would numb it. Maybe even kill a few of the poison molecules. Maybe take me out of my misery.

I followed Missy into the kitchen where she took two tall glasses out of the refrigerator, now frosted, then a rectangular bottle of Boodle's Gin and two small bottles of Schweppes Diet Tonic. All of Missy's movements were gentle and elegant as a ballerina. I was fascinated with the dance of her hands. Ice cubes filled the glasses, the gin barely reached to half an inch after cascading over the cubes, tonic filled the top. Then she took a lime and cut it into wedges with a sharp knife. She used a small press to squeeze the juice over the bobbing ice, and then put a fresh slice on the edge. She stirred it gently. Next the glasses went into metal holders with handles and then she nodded to me. A ritual not unlike a Japanese tea ceremony.

I followed her outside. Two chairs were in the shade of tall trees with a small table under them. Missy set the glasses down.

There was also a pack of cigarettes, the brand that's touted for a man's man. I knew where she got that habit from. But here there were no hospital rules. Missy shook one out and lit it with a gold lighter. It looked like a duplicate of Win's. Maybe it was. Mother and daughter matching lighters. I sat in what I hoped was an up-wind chair.

Missy drew on the cigarette and leaned her head back while she shot smoke toward the tree top. Win's movements with Sheila's face.

"Sure was a shocker, my Dad doing that," she said right off. "I just can't believe it. He really did one up on all the things I've done." She laughed. "He sure did."

I thought she sounded a little proud of him. I waited in case she was going to say more. But she sat, slid down in the plastic lawn chair and took a small sip from her drink.

"Yeah," she said, but that seemed to be all she planned to say.

"A couple of questions." I had a couple times a million. "Why did Eric go down to the store that Sunday?"

"Now that was a real kicker," she said. "Lord knows when Dad would have been found. Probably not 'til real late in the afternoon. Maybe even not 'til supper. Maybe not even until Monday, the way things were going around here." She paused for a moment as though trying to find the right words. "Somebody called on Sunday morning. I was in the kitchen, so I answered it. This guy asks for Mr. Loren Balfour. That's got to be a real close friend on Sunday morning, right? I just said he wasn't here. Then the guy says, 'This is the shuttle service calling to tell Mr. Balfour that we have to reschedule, so we will be picking him up one hour later. He'll still be there in plenty of time.'" She imitated the voice. Sing song, high-pitched. "So I say 'okay.' I don't know what this guy is talking about, but what the hey, whatever. Then Mom asked me who called, and I told her. She got all concerned and said we'd better call Dad and tell him. But he didn't answer at the store, so she sent Eric over there."

"No one had called for a shuttle?" I asked.

"Not any of us. I wanted to say to the guy, hey, come pick me up. Even just to the airport. Get out of here for a while. But I didn't. We just figured maybe a buyer coming in or something. Or even a customer. Dad did some really nice things for customers. Not my problem, though. I just delivered the message." Another stream of smoke to the trees.

"Off Eric went. What do you know, he comes back pronto, and he's like in Space City. He can't even get any words out. How he drove home, I don't know. Practically ran into the gate when he got here. He talked away like an idiot, and waving this piece of paper around, his hands shaking as though he's on uppers." She guffawed. "That'll be the day. Then Ma pulls him into the den." The cigarette strayed smoke toward me as if knowing I didn't want its amoeba body near me.

A piece of paper? I sat up, squeaking the plastic webbing. That fact rolled around in my mind with the others I already knew. Did Missy know the importance of what she was telling me? Was she, like Quon Lee, waiting for me, or for someone, to come along and ask the right questions so she could pass the information on? My mouth opened in exclamation, ready to ask a question, but Missy went on and my instinct told me to let her go with it.

She drank from the tall glass, sipping slowly. She bobbled one bare foot, looking at her red toenails. I thought of the maraschino red bow again, and the package. The Hawaiian scene her father had bought for his true love.

"Anyhow, I came out here." She took a puff of the cigarette. "Everybody in the family always keeps saying 'you're just like your Aunt Sheila.'" Missy said it with a nasal whining voice imitating the voices in her memory. "They thought that was a real put-down, after all she was up in Milford. 'That's what your Aunt Sheila would have done.'" She imitated the voices again.

"But I always felt that was a compliment. I was doing something different, not just sliding into the mold like everybody else in the family. They didn't change me with all that talk. Just made me more sure of who I was. I was different, like Aunt Sheila. I loved all the stories about her. I thought she must have been the greatest person when she was younger. I wish I had known her then, we would have been best friends."

She stared straight ahead toward the pool, cigarette smoke spiraling up.

"I wanted Aunt Sheila to come to my wedding, but they wouldn't let her out of Milford. She would have loved it. Not sure if the family was more shocked that my husband was black, or that he was Catholic." She laughed out loud this time, almost a guffaw. "Or that I was going to move back to his home. In Africa." She chuckled some more, but the sound had no enjoyment in it. She didn't sound as though she was enjoying being alive. I pushed that thought away. Was I going to come up with the right thing to say if she was in her father's supposed mental state? Would I be feeling guilty again soon? Like tomorrow?

"I loved it. Those were great days. I shocked everybody." She smiled a little. But her face looked sad. She didn't say anything for a few moments, lost in her remembering.

I started to ask about the piece of paper Eric had when she said, "My two babies and him were killed." The shift caught me by surprise.

Before I could produce any words from my banal repertoire, she went on.

"The other side killed him. Like the Democrats and the Republicans. Only if you're in the other party they shoot you. They didn't care that my babies were in the jeep, they just wanted to kill him."

She put the cigarette out, grimacing. "Friends got me out. Otherwise I'd be dead. I didn't want to go. I wanted to stay. I wanted them to kill me, too. I wanted to die. That's why I think it's so funny Dad committed suicide. Why didn't he tell me? I would have joined him. Father-daughter suicide. It's a funny world, isn't it? I escape death and come home, and Dad kills himself."

I didn't want to think about her pain, too terrible to contemplate. Far worse than mine. I'd only lost a husband. I pushed on with my questions, "Going back to that morning, what happened after Eric and your mother were in the den?"

"After a while I heard the car start up again. I just stayed out here, sort of forgot about everything, think I fell asleep." I glanced at the lounge chair. Didn't look that comfortable. "I just can't sleep at nights anymore. I have these terrible dreams. I really don't know what happened then."

"What piece of paper did Eric have?"

"I don't know. Something that Dad wrote."

"Did you see what was written on it?"

She shook her head. "I didn't see the words. He was waving it around, hard to see what was on it."

I took a sip from the glass not wanting to leave it untouched, then said, "Thanks, Missy." I leaned over and gave her a kiss on the cheek. She seemed to need it. And I had it to spend.

Whenever I had baby sat Eric and Bob, Missy was not in the house. Where she was, I don't know. She was older, a mysterious personage, going her own way, dancing to a different drummer.

I left through the gate to the driveway. When I closed it I saw her dive into the pool. Good form, little splash.

Then I wondered why two glasses chilled in the refrigerator. Hoping someone would knock on the door so she could invite the person in? Not me, particularly?

The one sip of the drink hit my stomach and head at the same time. I had to think about having something, maybe more orange juice. I should call Dr. Del and get his advice; otherwise I'd be on a drip like Marti.

What was upping my heart rate and making me a little dizzy, more than the drink, was the news that Eric had been at the store twice. I hadn't even considered that before. So Loren had died earlier. Earlier than nine a.m. when Marti was supposed to be there to meet him, sans luggage, for their trip to Hawaii via the shuttle to the ship.

The piece of paper. Not handwritten. A note from Loren?

Then I wondered if Marti had left a note. What kind of havoc would that have caused? But she had time to make it home to get rid of the note. And must have destroyed it before either Kirby or Lars saw it. If, indeed, she had written one. Another interesting, macabre question to add to those already marinating in my brain.

Chapter 25
Wednesday Noon

I went back to the office to contemplate some of my thoughts.

From what Missy said about the piece of paper, I wondered if it was the note Loren had written saying good-bye to everyone before he took off for Hawaii with Marti. Or a note to Marti saying he couldn't live without her? Heck, maybe it was just a grocery list.

It could have been a suicide note.

I had to know what was in the note.

Maybe Loren got cold feet and decided he couldn't leave Win and his life here. But he couldn't tell Marti that he'd changed his mind and wasn't going to leave. Did he feel he was on the horns of the dilemma and killed himself?

Could he have felt so pressured that he saw no way out of the dilemma—afraid to face Marti and tell her they weren't going? Afraid to keep living with Win after having found happiness with Marti? So he committed suicide?

That scenario didn't do it for me. Loren had made a decision, the biggest one of his life, and it was based on happiness. Going to Hawaii. With Marti. That scenario I bought. Maybe it was the romantic in me. It's the one I would want.

I kept hearing Cal's voice in my brain. You don't have diddly-squat.

Which brought me back to the piece of paper Missy saw.

I went to see Eric at the store. He could at least tell me what was in the note. He sure hadn't turned it over to P.D. unless that was info Cal had kept from me.

In addition, Eric was at the store twice, and that wasn't in his statement. I wondered why. If he wanted to set himself up as a suspect, those actions would do it. Negating that, however, was

Missy's description of him when he returned the first time, that of someone who was completely undone at finding his father's body.

Besides the two visits, I also hadn't considered that he had found and took a piece of paper with his father's writing on it.

But what if he had gone to the store, found out Loren planned to leave still opposing the Main Street Project, argued with his father, and killed him. I could buy a rage scene where he hit his father over the head with something or strangled him. But not that he hanged his father to make it look like suicide. No, that scene would not materialize in my mind.

Besides, he had gone to the store to take his father a message about the shuttle. Seemed a strange time to have a death-ending argument. Unless Loren told him where the shuttle was taking him—away forever. Even then, I couldn't see Eric that angered. But wait, what if Loren told him he was leaving them up in the air regarding the Main Street Project? Would Eric be mad enough to kill him? Would he be able to plan fast enough to make it look like suicide?

Nothing in the autopsy report about second ligature marks on Loren's neck which would indicate that someone strangled him first, and then strung him up. No fingerprints on the throat and no pressure point bruising. No evidence of conks on the head, either.

If an altercation between Loren and Eric had happened, and Eric had killed Loren, then why wouldn't Eric return home and tell Win that he couldn't find Loren?

Leave it to someone else to find the body. There were several scenarios Eric could have enacted—if he was the murderer.

I had baby sat him. I couldn't believe that kid in the faded jammys killed his father.

But now, the note. That I would like to see.

Eric sat in his office. I saw him through the glass partition of his cubbyhole. He stood up when I came in. On the closed door to my right was Loren's name and title.

"Eric, I have to ask you a few questions."

"Sure." His black hair fell over his forehead, making him seem even younger. I couldn't believe he was the grown up version of his kid self. I had the image of him, in my mind, curled up on the sofa watching TV and sharing popcorn with me.

"Tell me again when you came to the store that Sunday."

"Ah…9:30."

"I know what it says in the report, but you were seen coming in earlier," I lied. "What time?"

Eric looked at me without any surprise. "Maybe 8:30."

"And 9:30 was the second time?"

"Yeah."

"But you never said you were here twice?"

"Well, ah, no one really asked."

I sat down in the other chair in the cubicle. He sat also.

"I'm really curious, why didn't you call 911 the first time?"

He looked all over his desk, not seeing anything, for I could tell tears were clouding his eyes. "Dad was dead. He was…I mean…I knew he was dead…" He seemed to be losing control, so I switched tracks.

"You found him, then you went home?"

"Yeah." He gulped twice.

"He was dead when you arrived the first time?"

Eric nodded.

"You got there about 8:30?" The time my pink-shawled friend remembered the car driving out of the parking lot was 8:50. That also tallied with what Charlie had said. So 8:30 sounded right. Give him twenty minutes to view the radical change in his life, and then hightail it for home.

"Yeah." Eric looked down again and shifted in his chair.

"You went home. Then what?"

"Umm…then Mom told me to come back and call 911."

"What else did you and your mother talk about?" I said.

"Nothing."

"Did you talk about the note?" I held my breath.

"Yeah, well, sorta."

"Where is the note?" I said.

"Um, at home."

"What does it say?"

"Well, ah, not really a note. Not signed or anything."

"Where did you find it?"

"It was, like, in his pocket."

123

"In your father's pocket?"

"Umm, yeah."

"In the stockroom?"

"Yeah."

"What did it say?"

"I don't really remember."

"Think you'd better get it and I think you'd better march it over to the police department right now." I gritted my teeth. Eric had never been a problem child. But now I was about to lose my temper, his prevarication so obvious I wanted to shake him.

He nodded.

"Do it. Now." He was seven again, and I was his baby sitter. My patience slipped away.

I've talked to you and your mother, I wanted to yell. You've all played on my sympathy and told me all about your problems, your hurts. Not one of you has given me all of the truth. I've had it with the whole pack of you. The words were screaming in my head.

If he was any younger I would have ripped off the trap door on his jammys and spanked him.

I wanted to read the note to see if it held any evidence pointing away from suicide, but I thought it better that he take it to P.D. now. I could wait until later to see what it said.

I went back to my office, called Dr. Del to get the latest information from him. He had none.

I worked on my "to do" list and shuffled some paperwork; however Kathryn seemed to be handling the bulk of it. Maybe she was even handling Deb also. I didn't ask.

I had another thought. Perhaps they had sent such a high-priced secretary to check up on me. Was my job in jeopardy so soon?

Chapter 26
Wednesday Afternoon

My cell phone sounded.

Mother.

"Darling, they've just brought me home. Can you come over for a minute?"

Sure, Mom, I'll set my job aside, reading a possible suicide note at P.D., and come right over.

I went over.

"They're terrible."

I looked at the violets. My God, they were actually still alive, and even looked like they were thriving.

"What's terrible?"

"The windows. They're dirty."

Had she expected me to do the windows?

"You know how I hate dirty windows."

I knew how she hated a lot of things.

"I'm going to have to clean them."

Out of my mouth before I had time to evaluate my words came, "I don't think that's a good idea in your condition." Hell, she still had a cast on. "You'd have to get up on a step ladder. What if you broke a leg?" A little humor here because I caught on I was being set up. Snookered again. Point one for Mother.

An itchy feeling down the back of my neck. Did she want me to clean her windows? Now? "Mother, I've got to get back to work."

Too late. Her wrath was upon me. All that time in the hospital without anyone to spew her poison out. She couldn't take it out on the staff—Dr. Del would have found out. Must've been hard for her. I turned, hoping to sidle out quickly.

"You've always blamed me for Ted's death," Mother said.

So that's what this was all about. Finally out in the open. The windows to put me on the defensive so she wouldn't be. Ten points to Mother. I looked around at her tastefully decorated, always neat living room. Nothing I would ever achieve. Damned right, I blame you. If you had only—

"It wasn't my fault. How was I to know—"

"Anybody home?" Dr. Del.

We both froze.

She came back to the present faster than I did, but I could tell from her voice she was still angry at not being able to lay out her scenario.

"Del, you're early." Far be it for her to put an accusatory tone in her voice.

I turned. Had he heard? We looked at each other. I saw sadness in his eyes. Did he know I believed she was responsible for killing my best friend-husband?

"Hi, Doc. See you later, Mother."

I hurled myself past him, bumping into his arm on my way through the door, unable to say anything more.

Back in the car I gunned the motor, expecting to make a fast getaway. Hard to do since I hadn't shifted out of 'park'. I took off a little more sedately.

I went for a drive to think. My way of turning over a problem in my mind, drive and drive, mile after routine mile, along the coast, maybe stop at a vista site and watch the birds and the waves, maybe even take my shoes off and walk through the surf.

Ted and Loren.

Turned on the radio for some classical music and headed for highway 101, the top of the convertible down.

I wanted to think. And I wanted to be near the ocean, watch the breakers come in, the waves and their sound therapeutic.

It was where I had come after they found Ted's body in the twisted, crumpled car. In Mother's car. I had a lot to think about.

There's always a point where I turn back. I haven't made it to San Francisco yet on one of those drives. Probably never will. How many more drives will I take?

It was about 6 p.m. when I got back to City Hall. As I parked my car, I saw Skip in his office. I wanted to see Loren's note at P.D. Instead, I opted to ask Skip a few questions. I strode in.

"What kind of a deal did you offer Loren?" I said after I had honored the convention of etiquette.

He looked at his watch, glanced at his suit jacket hanging neatly on the back of the door, and sighed. He did still look fresh and unrumpled.

"We ordered three appraisals on each of the properties, along with an evaluation of the worth of the business based on tax returns, and then we looked at the financial records, and other factors. We based our offer on all of those factors."

"A fair offer?"

Skip spread his hands, "He finally got us up a lot higher than we should have gone. Every day wasted just meant the building costs would be higher. To answer your question—generous, as far as I'm concerned."

"But Loren told everyone he was being cheated."

"He came in." Skip's words were as clipped as his moustache and he leaned forward picking up a pencil. "Sat right there. I thought he was going to have a heart attack. He ranted and raved that his business was worth more. I told him that if all the businesses on that block were flourishing, we wouldn't be thinking about any kind of plan. No need."

"Did he counteroffer, give you any kind of a figure?"

"Three times our offer—that was his figure. Too much of a disparity for us ever to get together." Skip leaned back in his chair, stretching his arms over his head, folding them behind his neck as though trying to relax. "Between you and me, I don't think he really believed what he said about its worth. It certainly wasn't reflected in any of his financial records or the appraisal of the property or anything else we had."

"Why did Loren think that?"

"I had the feeling he was just trying to defend his manhood, lots of posturing, some of what he said didn't make any sense." Skip shrugged, dropping his arms and gesturing with open palms.

"The family was willing to accept the offer?"

"Were they ever. Salivating. They looked over the sketches. Loved them. I mean, they really loved them. They were excited.

They saw it as a way to turn the business around, make money."

I thought about the ladies' room in the old store, linoleum worn right through to the floor boards, uncared for as the driveway and parking lot.

"It's a smaller store?"

"Based on the usage of square feet, business tax generated, and again, other considerations. There's a formula for it. They weren't complaining about that at all. Eric and Bob saw that it meant fewer employees, lower overhead, more manageable, less inventory, easier to do a stock turnover in a shorter period of time."

Well now. Sounded like Loren told Mary Cordero a whopper. Had he been trying to make what he wanted into reality? What else did he tell people that was false?

Had I really known Loren at all?

I nodded, thanked them and left, heading for the P.D. office and Loren's note.

Sgt. Jessica Kidde gave me a copy of the note Eric had brought in. She winked as she handed it to me over the counter, saying, "Dace said you might be in for it."

I guessed she wasn't a member of the Dace Connor Fan Club.

I sat down on a worn leather chair in the reception area, afraid to read the single sheet of paper. Almost as dreadful as looking at the Polaroids. I closed my eyes and leaned my head back in the chair. I thought about the people I'd seen sitting in this same chair here in P.D. I was so curious about the note, and now I dreaded reading it. I'd been pinning my hopes on this note when I learned of it. That it would tell me either that Loren actually did it or that I had a murder case.

Finally, I put it into viewing range.

Dear Winifred

You know I love you and will always love you—but we've changed. We're not the same kids we were in high school. I don't know what went wrong. If anyone's to blame, it's me. I want life to be simple, but it isn't. I want to go back to when we were young, but I know we can't.

Forgive me.

It's all for the best—you will be happier, too.

The note was computer generated. Not signed.

It looked like a suicide note. Up to the last sentence.

If I looked at it as a goodbye note, the last sentence fit.

He hadn't signed it. Maybe interrupted while he was writing it. Took it out of the printer to hide it when he saw the person wasn't Charlie, arriving early for their appointment. Interrupted by the murderer.

Maybe he had finished it and was about to sign it when he was interrupted. The murderer saw it and liked the idea of it being a suicide note.

Maybe Loren didn't even type it. Maybe the murderer did.

Somehow by calling her 'Winifred,' the note sounded authentic to me. More formal because it was a serious subject.

It didn't read like a suicide note to me. It sounded like a goodbye-I'm-off-to-Hawaii note.

No doubt Loren's prints would be on the paper. And Eric's and Win's.

The murderer wasn't stupid.

He had done well all along. No evidence of his presence, let alone of the murder. Had the murderer known about the Hawaii trip, and that Loren was leaving town that day? Or was it just a fluke that he had chosen that Sunday, and not last Sunday, or next Sunday, to murder Loren?

My bet was that the murderer knew. But how could he? No one else seemed to know except Nicole, the travel agent. I had to find out who she had told, if anyone.

Of course, there were people Loren might have told but I didn't know who they were.

I didn't think Loren had told anyone. He certainly hadn't even hinted at it when I talked to him at the chamber mixer.

Had Marti told someone?

The murderer figured it out somehow. But how?

Chapter 27
Thursday Morning

It wasn't too hard to get an old Mirasol High School Yearbook. All in a row on a shelf in the Mirasol Public Library. Took me a few minutes to figure out the right year. They let me borrow it, and I went to visit the lady with the pink shawl. She looked at the pages of pictures of the graduates.

I saw Charlie's picture and thought he looked exactly the same, given it was forty years earlier. He had short, light hair which, now, had gone from blond to grey.

There were several pictures on the facing pages, but she IDed Charlie without any hesitation.

Charlie, you were at the store on Sunday morning. And the car pulling out of the driveway, that must have been Eric skedaddling out of there for the first time after having discovered his father's body. However, Charlie, if you were there when this lady says you were, you are in the clear. But if you made two visits, as Eric did, looks like you are in the running for Suspect Number One. Opportunity for Charlie as well as Eric.

Charlie, why were you there? And why didn't you tell me?

Charlie made it to the top of my "to do" list. I wanted an explanation.

So off to Palm Springs I went. Alone again.

I was getting madder. I had grown up with all of these people and no one was telling me the truth. At least not the whole truth. Who was hiding what and why? Protecting a murderer.

But if I couldn't believe they would lie to me, how could I believe one of them was a murderer? The plain fact was I couldn't.

As I neared the old Airstream's location, I geared up to tell him just pull that shotgun on me one more time, Charlie, and I'm going to...but I couldn't think of a threat dire enough.

By the time I parked on his sandy lot, I was so mad that the vision of his shotgun didn't even frighten me anymore. Anger had replaced fear.

I knocked on the tinny door again, calling out his name and mine. I thought I heard him breathing on the other side.

Finally, the inside door opened and he unlatched the screen. The shotgun wasn't in sight. I didn't know whether to be relieved or wary.

He gestured to the Formica table, and I slid into the booth. He set water on to boil, pulling out the blue tin mugs and milk. The steaming water raised the humidity in the small trailer to a stifling level. The hot air outside hardly moved. October in the desert. My pale green silk blouse became damper.

He put a mug in front of me and took a matching one.

"Charlie, I need to know the truth. You were in Mirasol that Sunday morning Loren died."

He had his hands wrapped around the cup as though for warmth. Maybe he was cold, but I wasn't.

"How do you know?" he looked at me with his watery eyes. The bottom half of his face had a light tan, but it still didn't have the weather-beaten look of the top half. He'd shaved the white beard Mary Cordova had told me about.

"Someone saw you."

He accepted that without asking who or where they had been. "It's been a year since Sheila died." He looked toward the bedroom. I hoped his thoughts were on the picture and not the shotgun.

"About a month ago, Loren called. Pretty much knocked my socks off. Only other time he ever called in all those years was when Sheila died. Said he thought I'd want to know that she passed on. I appreciated that." Charlie squiggled around on the upholstered bench like he couldn't find a comfortable spot. "But he wasn't encouraging me none to go to the funeral."

He drank some coffee and looked toward the bedroom. I wanted to tell him to get Sheila's picture.

"Then when he called me last month, said he had a business deal for me. That's funny right there. Loren didn't know peanuts about doing business. Doesn't have the head the old man did."

"What was the deal?" I was getting impatient. We all had lost loves and had pain.

He paused for a minute, then looked up at me. "Wasn't a deal. Not from my standpoint. He wanted a hundred thousand."

"A hundred thousand? Dollars?" Whatever story I had expected him to tell me, that wasn't it.

He gulped a mouthful of coffee and nodded. "Offered stock certificates as collateral. Willing to send me any kind of paperwork I wanted. I said no."

The mention of stock certificates started bells ringing in my head. The missing ones Eric and Bob had told us about at the Coalition of Ten meeting.

"Was he borrowing the money, or was he selling you the stock?"

"He never made that clear. Not that I asked because I kept saying no," but he kept calling, his voice getting higher and higher. He wanted to know why. Had to laugh. Asking me why. Him, of all people. 'And why are you asking me in the first place,' I said to him. You got all those banks in Mirasol, lots of rich folks up there, everybody knows you. 'That's just it,' he said. 'I don't want to get this kind of cash from anybody in town.'"

"Cash?"

"That's what he told me. Said I was saving his life. What a joke. After all these years, and I'm going to save his lily-white ass. Sheila would've laughed, too."

Charlie got up, turned the heat on under the pot again. He looked toward the bedroom again. "Got to get Sheila," he said.

I was damp with perspiration, my blouse sealed to my back by the plastic upholstery as it had been on my first visit. He came out with the picture and set it on the table angled toward him exactly as he had before.

Why would Loren think that Charlie would give him a hundred thousand? For old times sake? It reminded me of something I didn't want to think about. And didn't. I put it out of my mind.

But my shoulders were tense as Charlie set Sheila's picture on the table and gave her a small smile. The look on her face made it seem to me as if they were sharing secrets.

"Feel better if she's here while we're talking about her," he said to the picture. "Finally a week before that Sunday he told me he was desperate—had to have the money."

"Did he tell you why?"

"Never even hinted at it. I couldn't figure it out. Thought of a lot of reasons, maybe some business deal gone sour. Knew they weren't doing great with the store, but they weren't starving, either. Everything was paid for, the store, their homes. Wondered if someone was blackmailing him."

Blackmail. I rolled that around in my brain, not something I had considered. "He never said exactly why he wanted the money?"

"All he would say one time is that he wanted to retire. Didn't make a whole lot of sense, and I told him that."

"So you went that Sunday to take him the money?" I said.

Charlie nodded.

Why did Charlie change his mind? Then the topic I didn't want to think about sat there in the front of my brain like a big black bear.

"He threatened you with something, didn't he, Charlie?" He had no reason to do a favor for Loren otherwise. In fact, he probably reveled in being able to turn him down. "Some hold he had on you." Not Loren being blackmailed, but doing the blackmailing. "That's why you left Mirasol in the first place. What did he threaten you with?" But I knew. I knew it as well as I knew how Ted died.

"I can't tell you that."

"It had to do with old Mr. Balfour's dying in the car accident. You said you used to be a mechanic. You did something to his car." I was feeding on my own thoughts, brainstorming with myself.

Charlie started to cry as though he'd been holding it back for years. He buried his head into his folded arms on the table.

As I looked down on the top of his head, I felt chilled. Had he gone back to Mirasol, fooled around with Dawn's car thinking it was mine? Because I had come nosing around? No, there wasn't time. It happened while or before we talked. What if he called up a friend to do it? No, the timing still wasn't right.

I gave him a few moments while I looked at the smiling young

Sheila and tried not to think about her influence on Missy.

Then I put a hand on his arm. "Tell me about it, Charlie. The statute of limitations has run out, no one can do anything to you now," I lied. At the moment my heart wasn't in catching old Mr. Balfour's murderer. Probably no one even knew he was murdered. I only hoped Charlie wasn't considering covering all his tracks by doing me in, too. I had been ready to go once when I was in deep grief, but I wasn't now.

"Loren said he would tell everyone I queered up the old geezer's car. I wasn't trying to kill him—honest." His blue eyes looked directly into mine. "Honest. I just wanted to shake him up, make him suffer a little. How did I know he was going to drive up to Mulholland that day? He never did anything like that in his whole life, never went anywhere, just around town, figured he'd run into a lamppost or something. Didn't expect him to get killed." A grey handkerchief appeared, likely not its original color.

But that hadn't been true in Ted's case, I thought, and then shoved that back into the iron box in my memory.

Did you arrange for someone to tamper with my neighbor's car, Charlie? I wanted to ask. Did you cause the accident that almost killed Dawn's unborn baby? By myself out in the desert I didn't want to know the answer, let alone ask the question. Was I playing a dangerous game? No one even knew where I was. My curiosity and anger overcame my fear.

Charlie continued to sob, like a boy, into his arms. Was it because he'd finally been found out, or was he really sorry about the whole thing? I was now skeptical of everyone's emotions.

He wiped his face with the grey handkerchief. "Took it to him—cashier's check—that Sunday morning. Wasn't carrying that much cash around for anybody. Told him so. 'Meet me at the store at eight in the morning,' he said. Very specific about the time. Made me repeat it. Said he'd give me collateral."

Before Marti got there at nine, and before the shuttle to the ship was scheduled to arrive.

"But I got there late. Almost nine, door unlocked just like he said, light on, went into the stockroom like he told me to—and there he was laid out on the floor. No question he was deader than—" Charlie pulled the handkerchief out again.

That would have been after Eric left. Eric, who cut him down and laid him out, then hightailed it home to Mom to find out what to do.

I thought about the scene. It rang true, and I wanted to believe Charlie. Otherwise he was a murderer, and I was his next victim.

Small town or big city, Jo, murderers are murderers.

"Did you see a car when you were walking into the parking lot, maybe going up the driveway to turn on Main?"

Charlie thought for moment. "Seem to remember a car pulling out into the street, now that you mention it."

"Did you see who was in it?"

Charlie shook his head.

"What kind of car?"

Charlie started to shake his head but closed his eyes first as though trying to see it. "Yeah. Cadillac. Balfours always drove them. Liked to make people think the store was really doing good. Yeah, I do remember." He opened his eyes. "But I saw Loren's car in the lot, and the lights in the store on, so I figured he was still in there."

"But you don't know who was in the car turning onto Main?"

"No," he said.

"You said he was going to give you the stock certificates as collateral. Did you see them any place?"

"No. But I wasn't looking. I mean, seeing him like that and all. They could have been right in front of my nose and I wouldn't have seen them. Downright petrified. You never saw such a sight. His face...I got out of there as fast as I could, didn't want anyone thinking I had anything to do with it."

"Do you still have the cashier's check?"

"No, I turned that in right away. Didn't want to lose any interest."

"What about your copy of it?"

"Threw that away. Why keep it? Don't have room for a bunch of papers around here anyway."

I could verify with the bank about the cashier's check if it came down to that, but I believed him.

"Been sitting here every day asking Sheila why did he have me haul ass all the way up to Mirasol with that check? Just so's I could find him dead? Don't make no sense."

It sure didn't make any sense. The only way it made sense was that Loren had been murdered. But how to prove that? I put Dr. Del on my "to do" list. Given the possibility of it being murder, how could that have been accomplished to make it look like suicide?

If Charlie was the murderer, it seemed more likely he would have used his shotgun on Loren. Or me. Maybe that was the proof that he hadn't killed Loren and that's why I was still alive. Morbid thought.

Loren wanted the money to take to Hawaii. Had he made arrangements for an income? Did he have a pension plan? Maybe things hadn't worked out as he'd planned and he needed the money until he sold the store, the stock, whatever. Maybe he had just given up and was going to do what he wanted to do. Maybe he realized he couldn't stop the Main Street Project forever. Gave up and decided to go to Hawaii. With Marti.

Or just gave up?

Chapter 28
Thursday Afternoon

Driving back to Mirasol, I thought about how much sense it made that Charlie had murdered Loren. That way Loren couldn't tell anyone about Charlie being responsible for the death of old Mr. Balfour.

If Charlie knew how Sheila tried to commit suicide, then what better way to kill Loren? Like sister, like brother. Everyone would be making the same comparison. Simple, but brilliant.

Did he know how Sheila tried to commit suicide? He hadn't said, and I hadn't asked.

A good case could be made against Charlie in my mind.

But not in my gut.

I drove on the freeway toward home, hoping the lug nuts on my wheels were still as tight as they were when I left.

If he wanted to do me in, he could have put something in my coffee in his trailer.

Coffee. The taste still in my mouth, and then suddenly in my memory—

Kona coffee.

Marti had said she and Loren drank Kona coffee together every Sunday morning. Where in the store? They certainly didn't do it in the stockroom. I thought about the dust and grime of the years. Sure didn't sound romantic to me.

Where else?

Loren's office?

Loren's long-time secretary, Alison Walker, cardigan around her thin shoulders, unlocked his office door for me. I glanced at his name plate as I walked in. Sorry, Loren, I never wanted to pry into your life like this.

I surveyed the room. To the left sat a coffee maker on a shelf, vase on the table in front of the shelf, wicker basket chairs, and posters of Hawaii.

I could see them sitting there. Maybe holding hands, looking at each other, talking about Hawaii.

They met here on those Sundays. I was willing to bet on it. I pictured the vase full of flowers fresh from Mirasol's Farmers Market a few blocks away. Loren would have had time to go there and get them. Heck, maybe even Marti got them. And the chairs, the same kind that had been on the lanai?

A shrine.

I stood there for a few minutes taking it all in, thinking about them meeting, imagining their voices as they talked, their laughter.

I could tell Loren's secretary wasn't sure what the protocol should be at this point, so I said thank you and walked straight to his desk with the mantle of authority of the city attorney of Mirasol.

Now that I knew what to look for, the signs were everywhere. I saw little things from Hawaii on his desk—the koa nut letter opener, the seashell paperweight, maybe tokens they had picked out together or Marti had given him. I wondered what tokens Marti had at home. I thought about them looking at each other, in love, happy.

I peered at everything on his desk. Maybe expecting a revelation. A note. Dear Jo, this is what happened…

No hint that the owner of the desk had an intention of ending one life and beginning another in Molokai. Or anywhere else.

Piles of papers, the normal clutter of a working desk. Ugh, looked like my desk.

Nothing jumped out at me and bit.

I went to the coffee pot. That area certainly was neater. Powered cream and sugar cubes. Small wooden tongs, probably made from some native Hawaiian wood, sat on the lid of the sugar bowl.

Everything but Kona coffee. In fact, as I rummaged around on the shelves and behind the binders, no coffee of any kind.

They probably weren't going to have coffee that Sunday morning anyway. Maybe they'd used up all the coffee the week before. Maybe that was the timeline. No more Kona coffee, so off to Hawaii. No, that wouldn't work. Loren had bought the tickets far in advance.

Come on, Jo, you're getting a little giddy.

I guess love has that effect on me. Now that I don't have any.

No coffee. That didn't mean anything; the staff could have taken it.

If so, why didn't they take the cream and sugar, too?

I walked back to the desk and started opening drawers. I looked through them, all full of papers and file folders. Surely Eric and Bob had searched for the stock certificates here.

Straight down the hallway, through the open door, sat Alison, not too subtly watching me. I mean, she tried not to watch me. But if she looked up what would she see?

Hey, I'm not ripping off his paperwork I wanted to yell at her. I've got enough of my own.

I turned around. Behind me were open shelves with binders, catalogs. I halfheartedly moved things around, peering behind everything.

Then slowly, as though a revelation came to me, I turned around. Alison quickly bent her head. I stared for a moment. She had been his secretary for eternity.

I marched down the hallway and asked her about the coffee. She seemed taken aback that I suggested anyone would take anything out of Loren's office. Alive or dead. She said she brought Loren a cup of coffee every morning. The coffee maker? I asked. In case he needed to make coffee for buyers or customers he could. Where was the coffee he used for that pot? In this supply cabinet, she said. Would she get it for me, I asked. She stared for a moment, went to the cabinet and pulled it out. Not Kona. Just every day coffee, probably bought on sale.

I stood there like a moron for a moment. Her office, a long, open room, contained four desks. I looked back at her. I thought she was going to cry. I had dredged up people's memories, treaded on graves, and done all kinds of emotional damage to the world, for sure. And then as I looked at her my eyes strayed over her shoulder to the industrial-size safe, probably from the era of horse-riding bank robbers. Hard to cart that sucker off. The Historical Society would love it. My eyes lingered for a moment. Great place to keep coffee. Almost as air-tight as a refrigerator.

"Did Loren have anything in the safe? Something in a container?"

She pulled out a lacy handkerchief, brushed her eyes as she opened the safe. Not much of anything in it. Definitely no coffee.

I turned away, looking down at the worn linoleum. Darn.

Alison blew her nose and sniffled.

"Mr. Loren has a safe in his office." She offered this piece of information on a silver platter like a communion wafer.

My mind said, what? I turned and looked at her.

"I think I remember the combination. Did you want me to open it?"

I nodded, then marched after her.

Behind his desk and under his chair, a small area rug covered the worn carpeting. She slid the chair aside, almost reverently, then lifted the rug and the carpeting. A cylindrical floor safe. She put on the glasses that were hanging around her neck on a pink-pearl chain, then played the combination until the lid moved slightly. She stood up, fumbled for her handkerchief, and rapidly left.

I dropped to my knees and slowly lifted the heavy cover as if it was going to explode. My heart galloped so fast that my vision wavered.

Bingo.

There were several things in it.

Then, remembering I was an officer of the court, I took a pair of plastic gloves from my purse—one size fits all—and pulled them on.

Stock certificates. Two one-way tickets to Hawaii. A fat traveler's check wallet. $500 denominations, not sequential. Probably bought over a long period of time. That meant he had been planning the trip for a while. A business card from the shuttle service with a confirmation number and a time next to it.

I wanted to cry for Loren and Marti. So close and now so far away.

Everything Loren had told Marti was the truth. And more. Deed for the property on Molokai. Made out to Marti. Envelope for Winifred and one each for Eric, Bob and Missy. Win's was empty. Was the note, now at P.D., destined for it? Maybe the last thing he planned to do was put the note in, spread the envelopes on the table, take out the tickets and money, give the stock to Charlie, then off they were.

Affairs all in order. Time to leave for Hawaii. I looked down into the safe again, thinking it was the bottom, but was it? A plastic bottom for a steel safe?

I reached down, trying to get my gloved fingernails around the plastic. I pulled on it.

A can of Kona coffee.

Chapter 29
Late Thursday Afternoon

I called P.D. for an evidence crew to photograph, print and preserve everything.

I asked Alison if anyone else knew about the safe. She said Loren, actually she said Mr. Loren, had told her not to tell anyone. That meant Bob and Eric, who both worked in the store, didn't know. If they had, they would have found the stock certificates.

It meant the murderer didn't know, otherwise nothing would have been left. It was all evidence that Loren had no intention of killing himself.

It also might mean that the murderer didn't know Loren was planning to leave that day. He or she saw the note and decided to make it look like suicide. Maybe the murderer decided it was now or never, and that Sunday was the day.

I squiggled that around in my mind, but it didn't feel comfortable. Too much planning had gone into making Loren's murder look like a suicide. Not something done on the spur of the moment.

I was convinced it was murder, but I still had no physical evidence. Everything I'd found, such as the witnesses' statements, could all be explained away by a defense attorney. Heck, I could explain them away.

Next on my list was Dr. Del. I called him at his office and asked to see him for a few minutes.

His office was in an old building on Valley Boulevard near the freeway off ramp. The building was two stories, red brick, now weathered to a darker color. I walked in from the parking lot entrance, knowing his office was on the left. His door was ajar revealing him at his desk seated on an old wooden swivel chair.

He looked up as I slipped through the doorway and sat down. Nothing fancy here, a Norman Rockwell setting. He'd give me as much time as I needed, as though he had nothing else to do. I knew he had a full patient load in the office, his hospital rounds and what he did for the County.

I glanced down at the folder in front of him and read Loren's name on the tab. He'd guessed I was going to ask more questions about Loren, even though I hadn't told him.

"Tell me again about the ligature marks," I began.

"I stated in my report that there was just one set of ligatures on Loren's neck, not two. One set is consistent with suicide. Nor was he dead when he hanged. He died from the hanging, nothing else."

Now for my real question.

"If someone wanted it to look like suicide, could they do it?"

Dr. Del chewed on his mustachioed upper lip for a few moments. He looked at me and nodded. "It's possible. They could put the noose around his neck, but they'd have to hold it up at the same angle he was hanged. Choke him into unconsciousness first, then affix the cord to the tube. Have to hold the cord up long enough and with enough strength until he became unconscious."

"Could the scratches on his throat have happened then?"

Dr. Del nodded, but slowly, thinking about it. "I looked at my notes again," he said as he tapped the folder. "It could work, but the angle of the cord would have to be exactly right."

"What could you say on the witness stand, if it comes to that?"

"Just that it's possible."

Possible. Murder. But nothing that connected the murder to the murderer.

One step at a time, Jo. At least now you know it was possible with only one set of ligatures. That's a big step.

How did the murderer get Loren so complacent so that he or she could strangle him just right?

I went to face Mr. Personality again to tell him the good news. That I wanted him to work on a murder investigation.

Sgt. Dace Connor and I exchanged pleasantries.

Dace looked at me, actually made eye contact when I told him. Small mean eyes. Just my opinion, of course.

"Murder?"

"Loren Balfour was murdered." There. I'd finally said it. So it must be true. I heaved a sigh of relief. I felt a weight lifting from my shoulders. And my knees were wavering. I had to sit down.

Dace's dark brown hair was slicked back. Bear grease. His face showed that he was running what I had said through his mental computer. Should take a while.

I moved files off a chair by the side of his desk and sat down. My knees were now jelly. And I felt exhausted. That had been a permanent state of mine for the last few days.

I told him how it could have been done. How it had been done.

"Could be," he said. "Eric had the opportunity."

"Eric?" I didn't like the turn of this conversation.

"He was there that Sunday." Dace Connor bent back the forefinger of his left hand with the forefinger of his right hand. I was fascinated.

"And he had the means." Index finger now pressed down.

"He did?" That shot out of my mouth before I realized it. I was amazed that he glommed onto Eric as the possible murderer in the instant after I had told him it was murder. Did he know more than I did? What info had Cal left him?

"If you're talking murder, counselor, then the way I figure it somebody strong had to hoist Loren Balfour up." I nodded. "Eric was runner up in the all-state wrestling championship."

Dace almost came alive when he made that pronouncement. I got the impression he was more interested in the championship aspect than the murder aspect.

I had forgotten all about Eric's wrestling. I still thought of little Eric in his jammys. Great detective you are, Jo. A pair of jammys and you're all mush.

"If that's not strong, I don't know what is," he went on over my mental ramblings.

It wouldn't take Dace long to press down the next finger for motive. All he had to do was find out about the Main Street Project and the stock fight. Maybe he already knew. Then Dace would be pressing down on his wedding ring finger.

So, indirectly I was responsible for Eric about to be put in lockup? I had sent him over with the note. That's probably how Dace made the connection. Great going, Jo.

"I know you'll be interviewing every one right away. Need the transcripts sooner than yesterday."

"Counselor, I don't know—"

"This is a murder investigation, Sergeant." I gave him the list of names of those I wanted interviewed and what I wanted to find out. Didn't want him to have to do too much thinking on his own.

"You have the autopsy report?" I said. I wanted to see what it said about ligature marks, just in case the M.E. found possible double ones, even though Dr. Del hadn't.

Then I had another thought. The murder had to be premeditated because...

"I was just pulled off my vacation to fill in, so I haven't been properly briefed. Captain Elkhart's the only one to work the case."

We looked at each other, both of us irritated, but with Dace it was a permanent condition.

I leaned back in the chair, crossed my legs, and wished I could pull out a forty-five.

"Why don't you give me a copy of the autopsy report?" I thought I was making perfect sense. No reason to clutter up his pretty little head with facts.

Dace launched into a monologue about his partially-painted house, and the trip he was going to take with his wife and daughter and how they were now royally mad at him. Now he was mad at everybody in sight.

You know, Dace, I don't really care, I wanted to say. I'm tired, mad, disgusted and your problems bore me. If you stay in town, you know you're going to get called in.

I said none of it. I didn't have the energy.

He glared at me. Dace glaring is like Dace smiling. He pulled out the bottom desk drawer and fingered the file folders, looking at the labels as though they were written in Mandarin, then pulled one out.

The right one. Maybe I'd up him a point on the humanity scale.

The evidence of murder would have been a second set of ligature marks. Marks on the throat, somewhat lateral, made by the strangling, then another set higher and at an angle made by the

hanging. There was only one set.
     More diddly squat, Jo.

Chapter 30
Thursday Night to Friday 10:30 A.M.

Another evening of going home to an empty house and collapsing into bed. Dinner was an apple. Two pages of a book for dessert and then lights out.

I usually kept the cordless phone on my nightstand. I had the answering machine on in the kitchen, but if I woke up and was fast enough, I could answer it before the message kicked in. Anyhow, why did I care about getting messages? My calls lately were only bad news and emergencies.

To prove me correct, the phone buzzed. I leaned past the apple core and answered it.

Rachel. She practically whispered. I looked around. Who was listening?

"Got you in to see Cal. You're his sister Rose down from Montana. I reminded them about how good I am to them here in E. R. Some of their residents try in different ways to get out before their therapy course is finished. Tomorrow, 10:30."

"Great. Thanks, Rachel."

She gave me the details of where, how to get there, where to park, what to say.

So I became his sister Rose down from the Montana reservation, as Cal liked to call it.

He sat in a wooden chair on the lawn. Perfect picture for a Whitewater Center advertising brochure.

"How's the Chinese New Year planning coming along?" Cal asked as I sat down in a matching chair. Deck chairs for the Titanic. A small table with iced tea between us. Nice touch, I thought. Almost like home. Somebody's home.

"Good."

"Sorry I haven't been able to make any of the meetings."

I wasn't sure if he was trying to be funny or if he had finally gone over the edge.

"Cal, I need to know—"

"Missing the next one, too. Going to be up in Montana. Dedica¬tion of a memorial to my grandfather." His blue eyes looked over my shoulder. I wanted to turn around.

"No kidding?" Was he playing a game or telling me the truth? He seemed different. Subdued. Had he lost his sense of humor? Were they doping him up? Was that how they dried people out at Whitewater? I'd made a mistake in thinking he could help.

"Tribal gathering. Celebrating the festival of something or other."

"Some Indian you are." I paused for a moment out of politeness before getting to the real reason I had made an appearance. "I want to know if—"

"That I am," he said with that smile that turned a rotund almost forty-year-old face into a mischievous sixteen-year-old.

"I got in as your sister, Rose, so tell me—"

"That's what reminded me of all that. Sort of forgot about it. Forgot that and most everything else."

I turned away. Damn. Sedated to the max on whatever stupid stuff they give patients. I wanted to cry. I turned back to him, gulping down the baseball in my throat. After a minute or so, I said, "Tell me about Rose in case anyone gets chummy." Maybe I could get him to at least answer that question.

"Fifteen years older than me."

"Thanks a lot. That your idea or Rachel's?"

"Step-sister actually, and full-blooded."

"I don't think I pass."

"Hair's definitely a dead giveaway. Specially being curly as all get out." He grinned.

"No auburn-haired people in the tribe?" I looked around. Sloping green lawn. Looked good. Maybe I could move in. They could dope me up, too. Make me feel real good. I'd like that. I'd like that a lot.

What's it like here, Cal? I also wanted to ask. What are the sessions like, what do people say, why are they here?

The chair wasn't as comfortable as it looked. Maybe that's why the Titanic sunk. If you can't build a great deck chair, how can you build a ship?

"What were you going to tell me that night at the bank opening?" I finally asked him.

He looked over the lawn. "I don't remember."

"So, no great revelation?"

He didn't say anything.

Question asked and answered the first time, counselor, move on.

"How are you feeling?" I said, suddenly realizing I hadn't even asked him.

"Fine, fine," he said, nodding in emphasis, somehow not seeming like the same Cal, but rather like one a little humbled. But he was Cal of a Thousand Miens. This might be one of them.

"I've got to know what you think," I said. "All the things you haven't told me about the investigation. Talk to me." I could hear the frustration in my voice pitch.

"Jo, I've always wanted to tell you—"

A figure in white walking toward us. Our time had run out. So soon? "Quick, Cal, tell me."

"I'm sorry. I mean I'm sorry about Lily, about what happened with Lily."

Chapter 31
Monday Morning

Lily? Who the heck was Lily? I didn't even know a Lily. Was that a clue? Lily someone was related to Loren's death? Somehow I didn't think so.

I gave up trying to figure out what he meant because of the meds he was on. Disappointed and sad. No information and Cal a mess.

Maybe that's another reason the firm had sent Kathryn. To see if the billing was really justified because I was sure going over the twenty-hour limit.

To make the day even better, copies of the interviews the investigating team had done were on my conference table desk. I had to give Dace credit for moving fast.

Not in-depth interviews—each file only held a few pieces of paper—but now, at least, I could pinpoint everyone in time and place. Basically that's what I had asked for.

I was going to go through the files for opportunity. I knew their motives.

I hadn't ruled out a stranger sneaking into the store. But the premeditation, the planning aspect, to me, pointed at someone who knew Loren.

Means. Whoever did it had to lift up the dead weight of Loren's body, one hundred and seventy-one and a half pounds, to slip the noose of the electrical cord around his neck.

Win gave Eric an alibi—or proved her to be an accomplice, depending on how I looked at it. She sent him to the store, and he returned twenty minutes later with the news of Loren's death. Missy had told me that. What if Eric went three times, the first being earlier when he killed his father? With Win as an accomplice, then Eric could have killed his father after the call

Missy took. With Missy as a witness.

Eric's file went into the primary pile, Win's into the secondary. Win may have planned it, but she needed an accomplice to actually lift the body. An accomplice who had been a wrestling champion.

Whoever committed the murder would have a good alibi. After all the thought that went into planning the murder, he or she must have planned the alibi well. It was the murderer who got the electrical cord from the lamp department, not Loren.

I picked up the next folder. Marti. No verification of her movements. Kirby had been away and Lars stayed in his own apartment over the garage, so she had been in the house alone. No witnesses. I could have P.D. canvas the route Marti walked to the Balfour Furniture Store that Sunday morning, knocking on doors asking if anyone had seen her. But then she could have lied about losing her keys, and driven there the first time, then walked the second. Another person making two visits? I thought about frail, gentle Marti hoisting Loren up. But if I could consider Win had an accomplice, why not Marti?

Lars. He would have been her accomplice, no matter what she asked of him.

Say Marti went to the store first in the car and Loren told her he couldn't go through with it. She came home devastated, sicced Lars on him. Or she came home devastated, and Lars went to the store and did Loren in without Marti's knowledge.

Lars. The story of lifting the car off the man. I never would have guessed at his strength if he hadn't told me the story. Perhaps his devotion to Marti was excessive and he knew about the Sunday rendezvous. Jealousy? Did he know they were leaving together and wanted to stop them? What better way than to kill Loren? Marti wouldn't have been involved at all. Would he have done it, knowing he was ruining Marti's happiness? Seems he'd be more likely to help her leave if that's what she wanted. Maybe even kill Kirby if that would help her.

Lars may have been able to lift a car, but he couldn't lift that kind of complicated plan out of his head. Nevertheless, I put Lars' file on top of Eric's, Marti's on Win's.

Charlie. I put his on the Lars-Eric pile without reading it immediately.

Eric and Charlie had admitted being on the scene. Lars could have been. That gave them all the opportunity. Strength-wise they were all in. Eric a wrestling champ; Lars lifting the car; Charlie, though thin, worked in construction so he could be quite strong.

Kirby's file next. At a conference in Arrowhead that weekend, went every year. Yes, I knew that. His interview said he took a walk before breakfast and got lost in the woods. Plenty of witnesses who were in sessions with him afterwards. I read the interview again and started a third pile. He had a motive if he knew about Marti meeting regularly with Loren. He had the means, he was strong enough, but he lacked opportunity as he was nowhere near Mirasol at the time.   I picked up Quon Lee's file. He had told me he was there that morning, working in the diner. And knew Loren had arrived at the store. If he did it, would he have told me he was there at the diner that morning? I thought about the chickens he had hacked apart. He had motive and opportunity. Means? How strong was Quon Lee? Did he need an accomplice? Sammy?

Ah, Sammy.

I didn't want to think about that possibility.

Sammy's wife had just died of cancer and my Ted had died so we were two old high school friends drawn together by tragedy, just trying to cope for the moment. We'd had lunch together, talked about our high school days, caught up on each other's careers, but steered clear of our domestic states. We made plans for lunch again—not a real date, neither of us ready for that just yet, thank you. Our plan for lunch was put on hold when he was transferred temporarily to San Francisco to work on a big case. So he was whisked out of my life before he even became a part of it. He'd called twice, more or less confirming that the channels of communication were still open between us. We'd talked a long time.

Sammy hadn't been in town that Sunday that I knew of, but I'd have to check that out. Quon Lee went into the primo pile. I wanted to cry. He may have had the strength to do it, he had a motive and he had the opportunity. Also, he knew the timing, knew the door would be unlocked and that Loren was there. Could he have found another accomplice, not wanting to involve Sammy in such a sordid business? Would Sammy have cooperated with him if he had asked? Perhaps Quon Lee hadn't asked him, knowing that Sammy wouldn't be a partner to such a crime.

Shoving emotion out of the way, I realized that knowing everyone sure hindered me.

In my heart, I couldn't believe any of them had done it.

I sat for a moment before picking up the last file, looking over downtown, a row of palm trees in the foreground, symbolic of a southern California city. The sky was bluer than usual. Outer space.

Bob. Eric's twin and Loren's son. Camping and hiking with four friends all weekend at Big Bear. I dropped it on top of Kirby's file. No opportunity.

A chilling thought came to me as I looked at the time line. Eric arrived there at 8:30. If he wasn't the murderer, then the murderer might still have been in the store at the same time. Hiding in the stockroom or somewhere in the store when he heard Eric come in. If Eric had been there earlier, he might have saved his father, or he might have been killed, too.

I pushed the files away from me. All of a sudden this town I had grown up in and the people I had known all my life took on a sinister cloak.

Is that the way Cal, as a police officer, lived his life? Always seeing the dark side to everything, the evil that could be and the evil that was?

Or were they both the same?

Chapter 32
Late Monday Afternoon to Tuesday Morning

I spent the day drafting answers to pleadings, letters, instructions for Kathryn who worked like a magician. I thanked the gods again.

It began to get late, the sun setting when the door suddenly opened. I jumped. Twilight, but I hadn't turned any lights on.

Kathryn crossed the room and handed me a file. "Need anything?"

"No. Go home. Where do you live?"

"Glendale." Not far. She walked back to the doorway and stood there for a moment silhouetted against the light from her office, as though she wanted to say something else. Instead she pulled the door shut.

I looked at the file. From Dace. A tape in an envelope attached to the inside cover. An Acco fastener at the top. On the right of the file folder was a single sheet. An interview. Today's date. No transcript, so it must be hot off the reels.

Dace with Eric.

I listened to the tape. After the formalities, I heard Dace's voice change into a conversational one. My estimation of him rose at least two points.

"You were in the room when your Aunt Sheila tried to commit suicide." Dace said.

What?

I looked at the date again. Sheila?

"That's right, playing hide and seek," Eric answered.

"Who else was with you?"

"No one. Just me. I was waiting for Uncle Kirby. After school. But I had to wait awhile and there wasn't anything else to do. I hid behind the boxes because I didn't want anybody to find me in there."

"Tell me what happened."

"She..."

"Your Aunt Sheila, you mean?"

"Yeah. She came in with this thing wrapped up. She got up on the chair. In front of the desk."

"That's in the stockroom?"

"Yes."

"Then what?"

"It was an extension cord. A new one and all kinky from being wrapped up. Then she threw one end of it over the pipe. But she couldn't get it to go over. She tried to do it several times. Too short to reach the pipe, but she got it over the pneumatic tube. She looped it over, then pulled on it real hard."

"It wasn't around her neck, you mean?"

"No. Like she was just testing it. I thought she knew I was there and was playing a game. I didn't...." A pause.

"What happened next?"

"Then she wound the cord around the tube a few times and tied it."

"Tied it around the tube?"

"Yeah."

I could hear Eric's words coming faster. He sounded nervous, upset; his voice got higher—he was seven years old again.

"Then what?"

"She fooled around with it some more. Making the noose. I thought it was so funny. I had my hands over my mouth so I wouldn't laugh out loud. I think she pulled on it again. She tied it around her neck, and fussing with it like she wanted to make the knot just right. I was sure she knew I was there. Then she pulled on it again, but this time she stood on the arm of the chair and stepped off so she was hanging there. She screamed, but it came out all funny." No voices for a moment only the sound of the tape running. And Eric panting.

"I didn't know what she was doing." Eric sounded like he couldn't get his breath. "All along I thought she knew I was there and was playing this game. But then she's making all these funny noises and trying to pull the cord away. I got scared. All of a sudden I knew something was wrong..." Eric's breathing was choked. He lived the scene all over again.

"I wanted to go to her, but I couldn't move. I could only look at her swing and hear her choking. Then Uncle Kirby came in. He jumped up on the chair and helped her stand on the arm again. He got her feet on it. And then he took the...noose off her neck, and lifted her down."

Eric breathing into the microphone so loud it sounded as though it was strapped to his nose.

"My father came in and they talked about calling an ambulance for her, but she seemed to be okay. So Dad helped her out to the car, and Uncle Kirby got up on the chair and cut the cord off and threw it away."

"Did anybody know you were in the stockroom?"

"No. I wasn't supposed to be in there. I'd have been walloped. I've never told anyone about that until we went up to Aunt Sheila's funeral last year."

At that moment, the tape clicked off. I turned it over and put it back into the recorder. Nothing on the other side. I wondered it that was all, or if Dace hadn't noticed the tape ran out. Officially he should have given the time and his name, signaling the end of the interview.

Maybe the interview wasn't over.

A thought struck me. The chair. If Loren or Sheila was trying to commit suicide, why on earth use that heavy old thing? The store had plenty of chairs in various departments. Even ladders. Why not get a plain one that could be kicked over?

In Loren's case, it didn't matter because the murderer could tie the cord away from the chair so that it looked like Loren used it as his sister had.

The murderer didn't want to get another chair because he or she wanted the suicide to look exactly like same.

I picked up the phone and called Rachel at the hospital. "Can I get in to see him tomorrow?"

"Go about the same time. I'll make the arrangements."

"Thanks, Rachel."

The dreams that night were horrendous. One of them was about the woman in the red dress at the dance, laughing at me. Her arm around Cal. I felt sick, unhappy, didn't know what to do.

What did the dream mean? If anything. It left me feeling like a teenager, a mixture of emotions. I almost wanted to inspect my face closer to see if I still had pimples.

Suddenly, I knew who Lily was.

The girl in the red dress. Lily Carpenter. From high school. The night at the dance. I had wanted an apology then. Now I had it—how many years later? He remembered to apologize. Maybe they taught that at Whitewater.

The next morning at the detox center, we sat in a different place on the lawn. This time he seemed to be more with it. I brought him up to date, keeping everything crossed that he could discuss the case rationally.

"I've had a lot of time to think. Want to hear a theory?" he said.

"Hit me. I've got a few of my own."

"Someone short and someone strong who idolized someone so much he would do anything for her. And someone who doesn't have an alibi." Cal sounded like his old self, not on meds. That was a relief.

"You're describing Lars. So is he your suspect?" I said.

"Why don't you see if Dace will get you into the computer to see if Lars has any kind of a record?"

"Now why didn't I think of that?" I said. Yes, why didn't you Jo? "Explain why you think it's Lars."

"Had to be someone strong to be able to lift Loren up, he was heavy. Whoever did it had to hold him up while he wrapped the cord around the tube. That's the strong part."

"Okay. How can you deduce the murderer was short?" I said.

"Because he used the pneumatic tube instead of that pipe that's higher up and looks a lot sturdier. But he couldn't reach it, so he used the tube."

"What if he used the pneumatic tube because that's what Sheila did? And the murderer tried to make it look like Loren was imitating Sheila." I told him about Dace's interview with Eric.

"But Sheila used the tube because she was short and couldn't reach the pipe because it was too high for her. She was small, so the sturdiness of whatever she put the cord on wasn't important. I think the murderer was short, too." Cal leaned forward. "Lars," he almost hissed the name.

I chewed on my lip, probably getting lipstick all over my teeth. "You're thinking he's besotted with Marti."

"I think he worships her. I'm not talking 'in love,' I'm talking worship. No corroboration on his alibi." Cal tapped fingers on the arm of his chair. "Nudge Dace to do another interview."

"Nudge? That's not quite a word I'd use with him." Nudge. Sure.

"Get somebody in jail, then everyone'll be okay."

"Throw just anybody in jail for murder?" Was he on a different kind of meds? Should I humor him?

"Start the rumor—that's the next step," he said as though he hadn't heard me. "Get everyone looking at one person. Lars is the best bet."

"And get myself fired. And named in a lawsuit for slander. Thanks a lot, Cal. Not to mention a suit against the city for false arrest, false imprisonment—and slander. Then I'll be fired all over again for not advising the police department that they acted without proper evidence. Where will you be? Sitting here on your Titanic chair?"

Cal looked off over the green lawn and calmly drank his iced tea while I waved my arms around, looking like an inmate.

"Someone's after you."

"Me? Where did that come from?" I looked around as though for an assassin. Why did I let him get me riled up?

"Consider the attempts on your life."

I shifted uncomfortably with his statement. I knew I was in denial. Living my life like Cal's. His alcohol, my dealing with the attempts. "Why would anyone want to kill me?"

"What's in your life, Jo? Someone tried to poison you, got Audrey; someone tried to sabotage your car, got your neighbor. Find out Lars' movements during those time periods."

"How do you know all this? I haven't told anybody about Dawn's car."

"It's a small town, Jo."

I stared at him, going over the possibilities. Maybe the officer who took the call knew I lived next door. Maybe he told Cal about the fact we had—

"You're still carrying?" he said.

I took me a moment to switch subjects. Actually, we were still on the same subject. Me. I shook my head.

"You should. If you don't have a gun, tell Rachel to give you my back-up."

I felt my stomach swirl. "Even have this cute clamshell lady-type shoulder holster," I said.

"Go over to the range at the Department and get some practice in." An order. Cal was back in biz.

I looked away. I'd sworn I'd never carry again. The shoulder holster reminded me of playing war games with the boys. I didn't want to use my gun to kill anyone. Ever. I didn't like the smell, the taste, the feel of a gun. To me it represented a violent world, a world of people, if they could be called that, who didn't want to follow the rules of civilized society. A world of unhappiness, cruelty, spite, miserableness—

Cal's voice broke into my melancholy thoughts. "Don't do anything, Jo, about protecting yourself, and you'll end up like Loren."

"I don't have a new electrical cord around," I said before realizing what he meant.

"Maybe the killer will bring one. How about head in the oven or something like that. Despondent over husband's death, city attorney Joslyn Peters takes her life."

I gasped. I even had a gas oven to help them along. What's another suicide? Just a statistic. Would there be anyone investigating my 'suicide' as I was Loren's? Anyone who cared? Would Cal? What would Dr. Del think when he did the prelim on me?

White coats coming down the lawn.

"Tell Rachel to give you my backup. I'm not going to need it for a while." He stood up. Time over. He gave me a Cal smile. Then he fell in step with a white coat and went toward the building.

I stood up, too, and followed the other white coat who accompanied me to the gate.

"Bye, Rose," Cal called to me halfway up the lawn.

I did have a gun.

A legacy from my eight years in the D.A.'s office before Morrie & West of Century City.

Threats from gang members encouraged the D.A. to issue a memo stating the offer of free training and a gun allowance for those who participated in the program of self-protection.

My boss, Harold, a former LAPD officer, encouraged me to sign up. I'd never even fired a gun before and had never wanted to.

He and three of his cronies in our unit, all former police officers, took me to buy my first piece. My initiation into 'manhood.' I remember the five of us at LAPD's Athletic Association store discussing—actually they discussed—the merits of the weapons, cost, firepower and lots of other things that made me cringe. Hey guys, we're talking about killing people with these things.

Over coffee in the Academy restaurant afterwards they reminded me what the gang members did—the drive-by shootings with a four-year old girl dead, and a twelve-year-old blind boy now comatose. Wasn't I prosecuting gang members? Wasn't everybody? Soon I would be on their hit list, they said. Not a pleasant thought for someone who became an attorney because she wanted to help people.

They made it all seem so easy, having this piece of equipment in my home that had only one purpose for its existence.

All of them were so comfortable with guns. I think they missed the action from the old days when they were on the P. D. I knew they still carried all the time.

Continuing my initiation, they took me to the sheriff's department range, at which, because the D.A.'s office was part of county government, we were allowed to practice.

The hardest thing I found was not about hitting the target as I could do that, but stifling my own revulsion of the gun. It would never become a part of me, as it was another body part for Harold and the rest of the coterie.

I felt no solace in having it in the nightstand while I slept. To me it made a noise like a growl, emanating rays that rippled the muscles in my shoulders as it lay just a few inches away from my head. A creature alien to me and my way of life. A snake coiled ready to strike me before I could point its venom at the enemy.

So I put it away in the closet.

I went home, took a deep breath, and walked into my closet. I've got lots of shoes, but only two shoe boxes. They're identical, both green and white. The top one says silver, the bottom one gold.

The top one holds a pair of silver sequined shoes to die for.

I pulled the bottom box out and set it down on the bed. I carefully lifted the lid. Inside was a velvet bag, purple, the kind that usually holds a bottle of Crown Royal. It now held something more dangerous.

I pulled the gun out as though it were a sleeping viper.

Howard and the boys had recommended a nine millimeter Beretta. And that's what I had.

It fit my hand neatly and comfortably as it was supposed to. But I was not comfortable with it.

Gold-sequined shoes had been in the box originally. I'd last worn them the night Ted died.

Chapter 33
Tuesday Afternoon

"He's done time."

"You've got the arrest record?"

"Started the file," said Dace Connor. He handed me a sheet of paper as I stood at the side of his desk.

"Idaho. He was arrested in Idaho," I said reading the report. "Twenty years ago."

"Maybe he hasn't been caught since."

I looked at the arrest record.

"Stock theft. Embezzlement. Bribery. Armed Robbery. Interesting," I said.

Nothing about lifting cars.

Bad pun, Jo.

Dace nodded. Issue closed. Back to the paperwork.

"Lars' interview?" I said, holding out my hand. Knew they must have done another one after getting his priors.

He didn't answer right away. So much for our great rapport. I went through my routine of removing the papers from the chair and sitting down as though I was comfortably ensconced for the next month.

"Now, Sergeant, the interview of Lars. I believe you've concluded it. May I have the transcript? Or the tape?"

I watched his face tighten. Why does he always make it so difficult? Weren't we working for the same company?

"There's a problem, Counselor."

"I gathered that."

"After interviewing him, we've come to the conclusion that he could be the perpetrator."

"You're going to charge him with Loren's murder?" Had he been talking to Cal?

As long as someone's in jail, everybody's safe. I remembered what Cal had said.

"After reviewing the evidence—"

"Never mind, Sergeant Connor, I know the verbiage. Just give me the transcript." I gave him the sweetest smile I could conjure up under the circumstances. Dace wouldn't know the difference between real and phony. I wanted to ask him for the rest of Eric's interview, but I'd already given him two orders and I didn't want to confuse him.

He pulled open the desk file drawer and handed me the manila folders. Just like that, and Bob's your uncle.

And Lars is in the slammer. Maybe.

I went back upstairs, pulled off my shoes, let my feet whimper a little, and read the two files.

Lars' interview was interesting.

What was most interesting about it was that Cal had done it. Which meant before he had gone into detox. That's how he had known Lars had no alibi.

Thanks, Cal. No wonder he had such strong opinions about Lars.

I put my shoes back on, ignored the groaning from my feet, and made another trip to the clinic posing as sister Rose. Somehow I got in again. Sister Rose had squatter's rights, compliments of Rachel and her E.R.

An employee in a blue blazer and grey slacks escorted me out to the lawn site again. They must reserve the white coats for special occasions. Maybe a new public relations program. I wondered where they sent visitors when it rained. Did they have another brochure-type picture-perfect setting?

Mr. Blue Blazer told me Cal would be there shortly, and asked if I want iced tea. Of course, sounds lovely. Like it was the Ritz Carlton and I was ordering pool-side service. I hated iced tea. This was not the place to get too fussy.

Almost immediately Cal sat down in the large wooden lawn chair. Brochure time.

Before he even took a breath, I told him why I honored him with another visit.

"Everybody else is envious that I have such a caring family."

"I know you have nothing else to do for about three more weeks, but I'm in a tad of a hurry. I've got the firm on my back, the council, the Balfour family, the probate judge—"

"The probate judge?"

"Okay, so I'm stretching it. Tell me, Calvin L. Elkhart, why the heck you didn't give me information about the interview."

"I sent it to you in the inter-office mail."

"You know something? I don't believe that for one second. You hate to part with information. They must teach that right off in the police academy."

"I wonder if I could qualify for a police brutality claim."

"Cal, besides this little case, I've got a stack of paperwork that's threatening to sink the north side of City Hall. Now give about Lars."

"Yes, he's strong enough. Yes, he'd do anything for Marti. Bet he's a got a record. Am I right, Counselor?"

"Yes," I admitted.

"And yes to a bunch of other things, like no corroboration on where he was Sunday."

"So Lars is your prime suspect? And that's final?" I said.

"By the way, you probably didn't know this either. He's related to Marti."

"Now it makes sense why he's living with them."

"He came to town and asked Marti to take him in after he got out of jail. He's very grateful."

"One flaw in your scenario," I said.

"What is it?"

"The guy doesn't have the brains of a gnat. He couldn't have planned it."

"Definitely too stupid to have planned everything to make it look like a suicide," he said.

"What about fragile Marti?"

"As the brains? Possible."

"Tell me what else you gleaned from your interview with Lars that you haven't shared with the rest of us." I said it more out of sarcasm than any hunch.

"He thought something was going down. He saw Marti packing

her favorite jewelry just as she always does if she and Kirby are going to go on a trip. But since Kirby hadn't said anything, he wondered. She told Lars she had the flu and wanted to stay in bed."

"That Sunday morning?"

Cal nodded. "She might have told him that so he wouldn't go looking for her after church services or whatever was her usual routine."

"Maybe she made lunch for them."

"Whatever. She had to be sure her disappearance wasn't noticed for a while."

"We can easily ask her those questions."

"Funny thing. Lars said she acted kind of strange, not sick, more like excited. Can you believe this? He thought she was pregnant. If that wasn't enough to give Kirby a heart attack, nothing would."

"Pregnant? Isn't she about fifty?"

"He said she acted excited like she'd found out she was going to have a baby. Excited like that. Her cheeks were all red, he particularly told me. He sensed something was going down, but he didn't know what."

"So Lars hung around and watched?"

"Nope. Said he drove up to Bakersfield like he always does on Sunday to visit an old friend who's gaga in a rest home."

"You're kidding!"

"Lars said he spent the day with him as usual then came back."

"So he has corroboration on where he was at the time of Loren's death. You just said he didn't."

"I went up to Bakersfield to check it out. No one saw him there that Sunday." Cal rolled the iced tea around in the fake-frosted plastic glass. "They will testify that he came on other Sundays. He might have been there, but no one saw him—big place, busy, short-staffed. On the other hand, maybe nobody saw him because he wasn't there."

I sat for a few moments feeling the sun warm me, but still feeling cold inside, mulling over what Cal had said. "Did Lars tell you that because he felt the need to have an alibi?"

Cal shrugged. "That's my guess. Even if Marti said she saw him in the window of his apartment, which she could, she wouldn't be able to account for his every minute. And he only needed about fifteen minutes."

I shuddered. Fifteen minutes. Cal was right. Someone could have done the murder in that amount of time. No wonder I felt cold.

"Here's where we're at," I said. "You don't think Eric is the murderer. I agree with you. You think Lars did it. If you come up with the brains, I'll buy it. I've still got Charlie on my list, who's probably going to be arrested next when Dace finds out he was in the store on Sunday."

Cal looked past me down the lawn again. "What time is it?"

I glanced at my Mickey Mouse watch and told him.

"Got to go, time for a therapy session. Get to listen to everyone's stories as to why they were forced to drink."

I felt like yelling and swearing at him for leaving me hanging.

Like he always did.

Like he always would.

Chapter 34
Tuesday Late Afternoon

Lars. Right. I think Cal deliberately pointed me off like a bird dog on a wild goose chase to get me out of the way. Like a pesky kid sister.

Maybe that's why he hadn't given me Lars' file originally. Maybe that's what he meant to tell me at the bank opening, all about Lars. Yeah, sure.

I went home and fell asleep on the sofa.

When the phone rang, I had to claw my way out of a huge net. Struggling to consciousness, I dashed to the phone, stumbling as pantyhose and skirt had twisted what felt like one hundred and eighty degrees around. I grabbed the receiver and banged it against my ear.

"Counselor, I can't reach Charlie Quinn." Dace.

"Can't reach him?" Simple information means nothing to me when I've been jolted awake.

"No answer. I had the sheriff's department check. He's not there."

"Not in his trailer?" Suddenly I was in the current year, icy fingers down my spine again.

"Trailer's locked up. I authorized Riverside Sheriff's Department to open it up, critical emergency. No signs of a struggle either. Sheriff knows him, says his guns, canteens, sleeping bag, and things like that are gone. Car's still there."

"Off camping?" It was still light out so it couldn't be too late, but seemed like midnight. My body felt as if it had been in the path of the street sweeper. Suddenly I had an idea. "Did you find the picture of a woman in the bedroom or maybe on the kitchen table? Sheila. She signed it."

"I've got the deputy sheriff on the other line. She's at the site now. I'll ask."

Why was Charlie so important now? Were they going to arrest him? Or just interview him? How long had I been sleeping, a week?

"No picture. He'd take it with him?"

"Either that or someone wanted to make it look like he had taken off on a prospecting trip. Only they forgot he'd probably take the picture, too." I started to shiver.

"Do you know any other place he might be?" Dace said, genuine concern in his voice. Losing a case? Or a suspect?

I fumbled through the cobwebs for a moment, then suggested contacting Mary and Corky Cordero.

Dace signed off before I could say anything else.

My heart palpitated painfully. I was scared and I wasn't sure why. Was Charlie the murderer? And now he was off to kill someone else? On his way to Mirasol?

The other possibility that I didn't want to consider was that Charlie had gone to ground—because he had killed Loren.

Or maybe he knew who killed Loren. And now he feared that person would come after him. Did I lead the killer to him? Was Charlie spooked by someone? Is that why he skedaddled?

Maybe he didn't skedaddle fast enough.

Maybe he's already dead, lying in his sleeping bag out in the desert about to be food for hungry coyotes and other critters.

If Charlie's dead—I killed him.

In my bedroom, I pulled everything off, dropping it in a pile. A hot shower and then I dressed again, this time casually in slacks and sweater. I wanted to go back to the office and read those files again. I wanted to read Charlie's file again.

I pulled the front door shut, my hands shaking. The convertible top was up, but the windows were down. I got in quickly and tried to put the office key into the ignition. Jo, slow down. I dropped the key ring, leaned over—

A crashing noise left my ears stunned. A rush of night air.

Trying to identify the sound.

Familiar.

Nate.

Instinct kept me immobile. I looked up. The windshield covered with dots.

I twisted around, sprawled across the console and bucket seats. The back window gone. Definitely an improvement. Yellowed with age, and I couldn't see out. Had holes in it before. Rain came in. Now Jo, concentrate.

Sound. Torn fabric fluttering around. Part of the top gone. Night sky. Stars.

Purse. Lying on it. Gun. No round in the chamber. Clip...need to put it in.

A nightmare I used to have. Moving in slow motion. The bad guys catching up.

Ease purse out.

How much time before the shooter comes to check? Shotgun. Charlie. That's why he wasn't in his trailer.

Get clip in right position. Slam it home with the palm of your hand. I could recite it all for memory. God, I hated guns. Don't think about anything. Get a round in the chamber. Pull slide back sharply.

No mistaking the crack of the slide slamming home, thunder clapping into position.

In fact, there was thunder clapping.

The streetlight shone right on me. Would he come from the back and look into the vast hole? Finish me off?

Or would he circle around to the side? One blast through the open window.

What about the other side? Could I shoot over my head upside down?

How much time did I have?

Ears still numb, but I heard something.

If he got me, please God, let me get enough rounds off to finish him, too.

I couldn't see anything. So exposed with the light, and in an awkward, twisted position, my right leg going numb.

A sound. But the blood rushing through my head softened it.

No, there it was. Footsteps. Walking toward me on the sidewalk. Not trying to be quiet. Thought he'd killed me. Maybe I had an advantage. Steps louder. I was so vulnerable.

Louder. Steady. Someone walking. I saw a movement on the street through the now-open rear window.

White shirt. Walking steadily.

Figure passing. Saw it through the pitted windshield.

Footsteps. Fading.

Not the shooter.

I wanted to connect with the walker, yell at him, another human being. No. The shooter might blast him. Use him for a shield. Then we'd both be dead. If I didn't involve him, he might be safe.

Hurry, I wanted to yell to him, get out of here.

He passed on, his footsteps grew fainter.

I couldn't stay in the position any longer. The top of the console between the two seats dug into my back. I could open the door, slide out, crouch by the car. I'd be in the road. Surely the shooter was on the sidewalk side.

Maybe that's what he figured I'd do.

If he thought I was still alive.

Silence. Except for the roaring in my ears.

I had to do something.

The garbage cans at the curb. Maybe hiding behind them.

There was no concealment except the car. The street was empty.

I tried to reach for the door handle. I couldn't open it without sitting up.

A siren.

I waited. Please, come this way. Scare him off.

The siren grew louder. Coming my way.

Moments later the road was festooned with flashing lights. I laid the gun on the floor. I didn't want to get hit with friendly fire getting out of the car with a weapon in my hand.

I struggled to get up, pain in my lower back and numbness in my right leg. I opened the door ready to tell my story to P. D. so that the city council would know within the hour. And the firm an hour after that.

Maybe the rest of the town wouldn't find out until tomorrow.

Chapter 35
Wednesday Morning

In the office the next morning, gritty-eyed, with a small thermos of freshly-brewed Irish Breakfast tea from home, I plunked myself down at my wooden table.

P.D. had found no sign of the shooter. He had fired off the one blast. All the more to terrify me.

Dear God, just give me a boring day. No, make that many boring days. No more excitement, please, no more death. If I'm going to die, bore me to death. That's not asking a lot, is it?

My inbox had been stacked with a bunch of paperwork, but the one folder on top called to me, so I grabbed it first. A sip of tea as I opened the manila cover. Another interview with Bob Balfour, Eric's twin. In person.

Weekend in the mountain with three friends. Okay, that's the same. Then the reading got more interesting.

One of his companion hikers broke an ankle and the other two took him to the hospital while Bob remained at the campsite. I read it over again. Then the significance struck me. Each person came from a different area and met at the Ranger Station. Four cars?

And an hour and a half drive from Mirasol.

I caught him at the store just as he about to get into his car. He checked his watch but didn't seem to be in a hurry to evade my questions.

"You all drove up there in your own cars?"

"Yeah, Dick and Steve took Michael to the hospital and stayed there until they knew he was okay."

"How did they get Michael to the Ranger Station?"

"We drove down in my jeep."

Bingo, I wanted to shout. Instead I said, "Your jeep was at the campsite?"

"It's the only one that can handle that terrain."

"So you went down to the Ranger Station," I said, trying to prompt him.

"And we loaded Michael into the station wagon."

"Station wagon? Whose?"

"Steve's."

"And then?"

"They all went to the hospital."

"Dick and Steve and Michael? And left you with the jeep?"

"I went back up to the campsite. We've got a lot of valuable equipment, somebody had to stay."

"Did you stay?" I looked him in the eye. He didn't turn away.

"Of course, never left."

"What time did this happen?"

"Early. About five a.m. Freak accident."

"When did you get back to the campsite?'

"About six."

"You didn't come back to Mirasol?"

"No, why would I do that? Wish I had. Maybe I could have come here to the store and stopped Dad..." He choked on the words.

But you had time, I thought, and a vehicle. You weren't stuck up there the way the first interview read. Did you give that impression on purpose, Bob? "Anybody else around up there? Someone who saw you at the campsite?"

"We're off the beaten track. I didn't see anybody. No one saw me."

I let it go. He didn't query me why I asked the questions. Maybe he already knew.

He was strong enough. So now I had means and opportunity for Bob. Motive? Same as Eric's. What if he and Eric were in it together? I hated to think that. I dropped his file on top of Charlie's in the primo pile of those who had the means, motive, and opportunity to murder Loren. Forget gut feeling for the moment.

My cell phone sounded.

Mother.

"Darling, can you come over?" Maggie Ralston Peters in top form. I went. I'd almost rather face her than the file folders of friends who might be murderers.

I didn't have a good feeling about this. I was still questioning myself about why I had dashed to the hospital in a panic when I found out the paramedics had taken her there. She's your mother, that's why, a voice said in my brain. Not my voice. Maybe I had gone, hoping to witness her demise. No, even I could not say that. I was the only one to know her mother persona. Perhaps my father also, but I'm not sure about that. No one else knew the persona she showed me. Why? Why was I singled out? Her only child. I brought out something in her that no one else did or could. Had she been treated the same way by her mother, someone she never spoke of? What streak had I tapped into unwittingly? Would I ever find out? Would it matter if I did? Nothing was going to change. Even if she and Dr. Del married. Maybe he saw something, too, and that's why their relationship hadn't taken them to the altar. He was enjoying the good parts, not allowing himself to be ensnared by her into marriage.

Ah, Jo, move on, you're become much too introspective. All you're going to do is visit your mother. People do that every day.

Mother didn't answer her door. I walked along the driveway to her spacious backyard. There she was, leaning on her crutches, one leg plaster-swathed. She looked like she had a salt canister in her hand and was tipping a white stream out of it.

For a moment, I considered that she had gone totally, mentally stratospheric.

"Hi," I called. What was she doing?

"Hi, sweetheart."

I walked toward her. It was a salt canister. "What are you doing?" I could have kicked myself for asking.

"Pouring salt on the snails. It's the only way to get rid of them. I love to watch how they shrivel up." She smiled.

I turned and walked into the house. I headed for the bathroom. I knew I was going to vomit. Think of something else, Jo, don't think of the snails or any other wanton cruelty.

I went into the guest bathroom in the hallway, less of Mother's presence there, none of her perfume. I ran cold water over my hands and patted the back of my neck.

Think of cool waterfalls. Hawaii. Waimea. The flowers.

I scooped up a handful of water into my dry mouth and drank it, patting my lips with a pink tissue.

Okay, Jo. You can't live like this. There's got to be some compromise.

Spasms fluttered along my upper intestinal track.

"Joslyn, darling, where are you?" She hated the name Jo.

"Here, Mother." I looked at myself in the mirror. Who was I? Wife. Daughter. Professional. Widow. Alien.

I opened the door.

"There you are. Come on, darling. I've made some tea. Earl Grey." She smiled at me as though I was a shriveling snail. Making her way to the kitchen on crutches. She knew I hated Earl Grey. It has bergamot oil in it, giving the tea a taste I didn't like, a taste akin to French roast in coffee which I also didn't like. A game she played, to show who was in control.

We sat in the living room. Together on the sofa. My hands were cold and shaking. I held the cup above the saucer. I could taste my own bile and I chased it down with the tea that tasted like poison.

Mother was talking. About whatever. An African violet plant was on the table by the tea tray. It looked healthy. I was glad for it.

Her tone changed. She was irritated. Because she knew I wasn't paying attention.

She moved her cast-covered leg into my line of vision, using it for sympathy. Gloves off this time.

I looked at her. I could feel the muscles along my jaw line tighten, my lips grimacing. We knew each other well.

"It's still about Ted, isn't it?" Her voice low, controlled to a soft pitch.

I watched her. Waiting. Her show.

"Yes, I thought so." She sipped her tea. "Wonderful, isn't it?" she said, raising her cup.

She was trying to get a reaction from me, draw me into her orb, get back in control. Because she didn't have control now. If she got a reaction, she had control. Over me. Perhaps she thought with Ted out of the way, she might again. Ted was always in the way for her. A buffer. She had to get rid of the buffer. And she did.

"Let's talk about it," she said, setting her cup down. It settled slightly askew on the saucer. At first, I thought she might straighten it. Orderly. But she didn't. She put her hands in her lap. Mother trying to be contrite.

"I'm sorry," she said, "if you feel I'm to blame." Note, Jo, she didn't say that she was sorry she did it. I sat rigid, my mouth locked shut.

"I don't suppose telling you my side of it will make any difference?"

She didn't look at me. I was fixated by her mouth.

"You know, I've only wanted your happiness."

Lying mouth.

"Every mother wants that for her children."

But she wasn't that kind of mother.

She took a breath. I could tell she was calculating how much of a whopper she was going to tell next. How much would I swallow? She rubbed her cast, underlining her temporary disability.

"And when you married Ted, I was very pleased. For you. I know you were very happy with him."

Happy with him, and no longer attentive to Mother. And she'd found out very quickly she couldn't control Ted.

"I am truly, terribly sorry." She turned to me, her blue eyes glistening with tears.

The whopper was coming.

I set my cup and saucer down. Cold tea splashed over my hand.

I got up, knees shaky, wobbling in my high heels on the plush carpeting. I staggered around the coffee table and headed for the front door.

"I didn't kill him," she called after me.

At the curb, I threw up in the gutter. Just as I had over my gold-sequined shoes when I had been informed that Ted died in an accident on the winding mountain road after doing her a favor by driving Maggie Ralston Peters' power fluid and brake fluid-dry Mercedes convertible from her French Chateau-style house on the lake in Big Bear back to Mirasol. Ted never made it back. Back to me.

Chapter 36
Later

I drove and drove. The time just went. I stopped for an early dinner. I don't even remember what I ate. Or where. Good thing I didn't need an alibi. Then I headed back to Mirasol. Spent. Which is what I wanted to feel so I'd be too tired to think about some things.

I wanted to get my mind off how sorry I felt for myself. Go back to work, I told myself.

I decided to see Marti again. Maybe find out if whether Loren had told her anything about giving up the fight against the Main Street Project, for that's what the notes to his children had said. They were to send him his share of the sale.

At the hospital, I learned she had been released. Perfect terminology as far as I was concerned.

Heading towards the Hawkins' house, I suddenly became aware of all the people on the streets. Seemed like more than usual for early evening, but I really didn't think too much about all the darting figures. When I parked in front of Marti's house, I saw the small ghosts and goblins and other costumed figures. Halloween. I'd forgotten all about it.

I knocked at the door of Kirby and Marti Hawkins' brick ranch-style house.

Kirby opened the door with a bag of candy corn kernels in one hand. "Hi," I said. "I came to see Marti."

"Come on in." Kirby pumped my hand.

It was a comfortable room and I had my choice of the sofa or two overstuffed chairs. The latter looked like they were hard to get out of. A rocking chair on one side of the fireplace had a book spread-eagled on the seat. Coffee mug nearby. I chose the end of the sofa away from it, facing the dead fireplace.

"Coffee, soft drink?" Kirby smiled over me.

"Water would be fine." I suddenly realized how thirsty I was after the long drive.

He brought it to me and set down on the end table a small tray that held an opened bottle of water, a glass full of ice and a napkin. What lovely service. I told him so.

He nodded. I expected him to get Marti, but he didn't. Instead he moved his book and sat down on the rocker.

The doorbell chimed. He didn't move. We looked at each other for a moment, then I turned away and poured the water over the ice cubes into the glass. The crackling and whooshing sounds interspersed with the doorbell chiming. I wondered what Kirby planned to do with all those candy corn kernels.

"What did you want to see Marti about?"

I glanced across to him. He wasn't smiling anymore. Bonhomie gone.

Doorbell.

"I'm going to turn off the porch light." He went into the hallway. I heard him greeting the new batch of trick-or-treaters, and the snap of the lock as the door closed shut.

"We shouldn't be bothered now."

"I want to talk to Marti. I have some questions for her."

"Why do you continue to bother her? She knows nothing—"

"I just want to see how she's feeling."

"She's feeling fine."

"I need to see her, Kirby. Now."

"No, she's resting."

"I'll only be a few minutes."

"It's all right, Kirby."

We both gasped at the sound of Marti's voice.

"Go back to bed, Marti. You need to rest."

"No more orders, Kirby. That was our agreement."

My eyes swiveled back and forth in tennis-match style between Marti, who was in the doorway behind the sofa and Kirby, about to rise from the rocker.

"This doesn't concern you," he said to her.

"Marti," I said, feeling the tension between them like lightning flashes, "I have a couple of questions. I'll come into the bedroom with you if you want to lie down."

"I'm tired of being treated like a child." Marti to Kirby, neither of them looking at me. Looks exchanged between them. Outside, voices and laughter bubbled from little ghosties and goblins. I wished I was one of them. I wished I was home answering my door to them, giving them candy, doing normal things. Doing normal things. That's why I had left the D.A.'s office, so I could hand out candy to normal kids dressed liked ghosties and goblins.

I turned further, now sitting sideways on the sofa, fascinated by the drama, my hand knocking over a glass paperweight of Westminster Abbey. I straightened it. Now it was snowing in London.

London.

Kirby knowing which direction was which, even underground.

I gasped. "You weren't lost in the woods. You couldn't get lost." The words came out of my mouth before I had a chance to stop them.

His eyes snapped to me.

I tried to remember the timing. Not Bob making it to Mirasol. Kirby. "You had enough time to drive here and back."

"No! I was lost. Wandered around for—"

"Hours," I said. "You wandered around for hours. That's what you told them at the conference when they asked where you were. You said that in your interview. No one saw you for hours that morning. Time enough to drive to Mirasol, kill Loren and drive back."

"What!" Marti said.

"That's not true." Kirby's glance darted between us, his eyes dark. "Loren committed suicide." This to Marti.

"Loren was murdered," I said.

"Loren was...murdered? You mean, he didn't commit suicide. He didn't..." Her face was a study of incredulousness.

The news was a surprise to Marti. I noticed it didn't seem to be news to Kirby. But then rumors fly fast in a small town, maybe he'd heard. And then again, maybe not. His eyes darted back and forth between Marti and me. Don't say anything else, his eyes seem to be saying, at the same time he was afraid I was going to say something else. And I did.

"Loren did not commit suicide," I said this to Marti.

I worked it out as I talked.

"Loren committed suicide," Kirby said as though reading a script. "He was unstable just like his sister. It runs in the family. Why, he even did it exactly the same way. Exactly."

Then I knew for sure.

"You," I said to Kirby, gasping at my own realization. It couldn't be. "You were the only one who knew exactly how Sheila tried to commit suicide. You imitated that."

"That's common knowledge. Everybody knows." Kirby's words gushed.

"No. Only you knew. You were the one to cut her down. You would have noticed. Perhaps even asked Eric about what he saw when he was hiding in the storeroom."

"That's not true. Marti, don't listen to her. Go back into the bedroom."

"It's true," I said. "Eric never told anyone." I spaced the words out emphasizing their importance to myself.

I pressed on, horrified at what I was thinking, playing the scenario out as I talked. "Eric never told anyone until the day of his Aunt Sheila's funeral. You said he rode up with you. I'm betting Marti sat in the front seat with Lars driving, and you and Eric in the back. Maybe you got him talking about the day she tried to do herself in. Maybe you wanted some more details. So that you could say, just as you did, that it runs in the family. Only you didn't know that Eric hadn't told anyone. It was his guilty secret.

"Maybe that's what gave you the idea. Because somewhere along the line you learned that Marti was leaving you for Loren."

The look on his face, not one of denial, told me more than I wanted to know.

"It had to be you. You had the motive—how could any man stand to be rejected like that, and supplanted by your best friend—"

"Quiet!"

But I wasn't. "You had the means, you're definitely strong enough. And you had the opportunity. You drove back here, killed him and returned to the conference."

"I think you'd better leave. You're upsetting Marti." Kirby took a step toward me. "I'm sorry to learn that you're as unstable as Loren was."

Marti, wide-eyed, looked beyond upset. Transfixed. Shocked. Horrified. Feeling all the things I would probably feel if I found out my husband had killed the only man I had ever been in love with. All the things I felt about my mother.

"What are you going to do, Kirby? String me up? I'm telling the truth about you. I can't believe it. You must have really hated him."

"You must have known they were planning to leave that day. Just as Lars did. Maybe you also saw her pack her jewelry. Something. You knew that Sunday was going to be different. But they had planned it knowing you were going to be at the conference and not back until late. After they'd gone." I was talking slowly, feeling my way, picturing in my mind the scenario, sensing how it could have been.

"No!" Kirby's negative was explosive. I jumped. He looked torn, angry with me, yet trying to calm Marti, convince her I was lying. In her white, ethereal nightgown, she sidled to the desk. I thought she wanted to collapse in the chair there, for she leaned heavily on the desk as soon as she touched it.

"Lars." They both looked at me. "That's why you had Lars tell me that story about how strong he was. You knew I'd be looking for someone strong as a suspect."

"Marti, don't! It's lies, all lies."

Then another cold thought hit me. "I can't believe you did this. But you planned it so that Marti would find him. Her punishment for those Sunday morning meetings. It was Marti who was supposed to find him. If she had followed her regular schedule..." I thought of the monstrous cruelty. Not only killing Loren, but making Marti suffer further by finding his body like that.

What did he think? That Marti would be grateful to still have him after Loren died? Maybe he would comfort her. Try to make up for murdering Loren?

"I hope they put you away for a long time, Kirby."

His attention was diverted to Marti opening the desk drawer.

What Marti went to the desk for, she now had. A gun.

I thought about mine. In the car, snapped in its cute clamshell holster, locked in the glove compartment.

Why hadn't Kirby tried to stop her from getting the gun? Because I was there? Because he had hurt her enough? Because he didn't believe Marti would use it? I didn't either. Did she even know how to use it?

I watched her as though we were in a movie. We were the movie. She held the gun, her arm stiff, taking a few steps toward Kirby.

"Marti, don't," I said, standing. Could I get the gun away from her? I'd have to leap over the back of the sofa.

Kirby sprang, pushing her arm and the gun toward me.

A flash.

My ears deadened.

Stuffing erupted from the sofa where I had been sitting.

I looked at it. Dazed. Kirby had deliberated knocked the gun in my direction? That stuffing would have been my insides. That's why he let Marti get the gun; he was hoping to do serious damage to my body. And then blame it on Marti. Maybe even twist the gun in her hand so that she too died, and looked like a suicide. All these thoughts fast forwarded as I watched them, completely paralyzed, only my mind working.

A second shot.

Red poured from Kirby's neck like a fountain.

He jerked, stopped by the rocker. His body bent backwards over it. He reached out to grip the arm, and stayed suspended in that position for what seemed like minutes.

Then he slipped to the floor. Face up. Head cracking on the tile hearth.

I heard glass breaking. I couldn't take my eyes off Kirby. The sound of the gun and the redness of the blood made me feel faint, paralyzed. The trauma of Nate's death all over again. I felt hot, the floor wavering before my eyes.

Cal. In the doorway of the living room in official police stance, crouched with gun extended in both hands.

He had a puzzled look on his face.

It took me a moment to realize that Cal couldn't see the gun in Marti's hand for a white fold of her nightgown covered it. Nor could he see the body. But he had heard two gunshots, and the man was not stupid.

Then he saw Kirby prone, and looked at my empty hands.

Cal went up to Marti, and slipped the gun out of her hand. Then helped her onto the chair by the desk. He used the phone in the hall to call for the DB team. I heard him say 'accident.' I backed away from the shredded sofa onto the chair in the corner by the window.

Cal came back with two glasses of amber liquid. He gave Marti one. "It's good. Martell's. New bottle." As though he was our host.

Then he came over to me, his eyes their clearest light blue, he looked as though he was going to hand me the glass, but he put it on the end table. And for thirty seconds Mirasol High's football captain held me to him.

"How..." I started to ask while the Dead Body Team worked in the living room. We were across the hall in the dining room.

"Would you believe I got a subpoena, have to testify in court tomorrow? The judge didn't take too kindly to the chief saying I was unavailable and wouldn't be there, especially when she had to tell the judge where I was. So they let me out. Have to go back afterwards." He had a slight smile on his face. "Stopped by the office to pick up the file, then I was on my way home. I saw your car and wondered why you were here. I started putting two and two together. I thought maybe it had to do with Lars. But before I figured it all out, I heard the shot and broke in expecting to find your O negative all over." He grinned. "Simple as that, ma'am."

"I wanted to talk Marti again. Once I was here I wondered why Kirby was trying to stall me. He had to have a reason. He didn't want Marti to find out anything I could tell her. It wasn't that he didn't want me to ask Marti questions. I kept wondering why. Then suddenly I remembered about Kirby's sense of direction. And the fact that he was the only one who knew how Sheila tried to commit suicide and it all fell into place."

Cal shook his head. "I can't believe you came here all alone. And then you left your gun in the car. You didn't listen to me."

"I didn't know I was walking into the home of a murderer."

"Tell me all about it."

"I'll send you my report in the inter-office mail," I said.

Chapter 37
Later

I told Cal I was exhausted and I wanted to go home. I was bone-tired from answering questions. We were just hanging around on the periphery while everything was being photographed, written up, bagged—all the movements of the death ballet.

"I'll walk you to your car." Outside, when he saw the strips from the fabric roof of my car laying haphazard on the trunk, he said, "What happened? It looks like a real ragtop now."

"That sounds like a good title for a song." I told him what happened. "It just got a little worse driving around today."

"You think Kirby did that?"

"I'm thinking Charlie. He's not at his home in Palm Springs." I related Dace's call.

"But why?"

I brought him up to date on old Mr. Balfour's death.

"You think Charlie tried to kill you because you knew about the old murder?"

"I don't want to believe it. But he does have a shotgun."

"Explain the poisoning and your neighbor's car tampering."

"Had to be Kirby doing the poisoning. He has access to City Hall, knows where my office is. No one would think twice if they saw him there. Like you said, the murderer knew I was asking too many questions. The car," I shrugged, "could be juvies up to no good. Purely coincidence."

A time beat. Then he said, "Rachel wants a divorce."

"What?" I stopped and looked at him. "You mean now that you're all cured? When did she tell you?"

"She didn't actually come right out and say it. She just sort of said—"

"Maybe you're reading her wrong."

"I'm more tuned in now that I've got a clear head. I guess it's been there, maybe that's why—" He stopped, and looked up at the stars.

"Maybe that's why what?"

"Forget it, you're tired. Get some sleep. I'll talk to you tomorrow."

I remembered the last time he said that at the bank opening, and then the next day he was in detox. "I'll be all right after I have some tea. Why don't you come over for a cup?" Why had I asked him? I knew. I didn't want to be alone. But did I want to be with Cal?

He followed me home, just a few blocks away. I parked in front of the house, too tired to bother putting the car away. I remembered to take the gun out of the glove compartment, left the clamshell holster, and slipped it into my jacket pocket.

Cal offered to put the car in the garage, convincing me that leaving it on the street in that condition didn't seem the practical thing to do on Halloween night. "Okay, okay," I said, and slipped the car key off my key ring. "I'll put the water on to boil."

"I take mine black," he said.

I unlocked the front door and went in, leaving it open for Cal. I walked down the hallway into the living room and turned on the light.

I smelled him before I saw him.

Sonnyboy. Shotgun at the ready.

I heard myself gasp.

"Hello there, Miss Big-time Lawyer."

"Leroy." His face was covered with thick white paint as though it had been applied with a palette knife. Around his eyes, his mouth, and on his hair was some sort of black substance like tar. I would have been frightened seeing him even if I hadn't recognized him. Perfect for Halloween. No one would think twice about this ghoul. Just a little bigger than most, but not by much. And no one would be able to identify him later.

I looked at the shotgun again. All my fears and nightmares suddenly came to fruition.

Then it became clear.

The unanswered questions about Kirby. "You're the one who

poisoned us and caused the accident with my neighbor's car. You're the one who shot at me."

"You got away from me the other night. So I came back to make sure this time."

"Tell me why you're trying to kill me. Why did you kill Nate? We got you off."

"You both laughed at me," he said.

"We did not. What are you talking about?" I said.

"You both thought I was funny. You were always throwing sand in my face."

"Throwing sand?"

"Treating me like I'm a crazy, like I didn't know what I was doing, like shooting that guy in the store was wrong. A real jerk, he didn't deserve to live. He threw sand in my face, too."

I wanted to say 'stop, you're not making any sense.' But then he was crazy, he wasn't supposed to make sense. Maybe I was crazy for trying to have a conversation with him. As crazy as him.

I had a gun in my pocket.

"Get in here, Miss Smarty Lawyer. Sit down."

Could I be faster than his shotgun? He was younger, quicker. Crazier. I might get shot, but I was going to take him with me and I was going to keep firing even though my head burst like a watermelon as Nate's had.

"And you were sleeping with him. You, a white broad, how could you do that?'

I laughed, guffawed actually. Mistake. The gun came up. "Wait," I said. "Nate was a homosexual. No way were we sleeping together." He looked dubious. "Honest," I said, holding up my left hand like a girl scout. Waving it to get his eyes. Right hand sliding into my pocket.

"Good thing I blew him away, yeah, man, another one bites the dust." He laughed.
I shifted, turning slightly away, feeling the gun. It was barrel up in my pocket. How had I managed to do that?

"You sicced the cops on me. If you'd've kept your mouth shut, they wouldn't be hunting for me. But no, Miss Lawyer Bitch has to blab all over who did it. I get rid of you, nobody to say they saw me do it."

I didn't have a devious enough mind to figure out what he was talking about or come up with any logic that would appeal to him, if any. I tried to turn the gun around in my pocket.

"What are you doing?" He came closer.

"Want me to make some tea?" I blurted thrusting out my left hand again, away from me, as though proffering him a tea cup and saucer.

"Tea. Are you crazy or something? You think I came here for tea?" He laughed again. "You're really something, Miss Bitch Lawyer." The smile went from his face. This was it.

"Wait," I said, "I have one more question."

"Don't have time for any." He raised the shotgun higher.

I had my finger on the trigger.

He clicked off the safety.

I fired.

Sonnyboy jerked. The shotgun went off over my left shoulder, shattering the plaster on the wall. I hit the floor firing all my rounds at him. The shotgun went off again, burning a hole in the carpet. I kept pulling the trigger as though I was holding a Raid can on a moving cockroach.

"He's dead, Jo." Cal came in, his gun at the ready, and kicked the shotgun out of his hands. Sonnyboy's body spasmed, and then it lay still.

"Think you missed him a few times," Cal said.

"I don't know how, he's only about two feet away from me."

"You were kind of shaking, like spraying him with bullets."

"What were you doing? Where were you for so long?"

"Wasn't sure who he was at first. Thought maybe a boyfriend. Sounded like you two were having a little friendly conversation. Your voice sounded different. That's why I didn't say anything. I was going to take off."

"I shot him through my brand new Liz Claiborne jacket. Paid full price, too. Wasn't even on sale."

"Sure looks like your car top now. I can hear everybody when I call in for another DB team. They're going to think I'm kidding." Cal looked around and found the phone. I walked out into the hallway. I didn't want to be in the same room with Sonnyboy's body.

Cal kept an eye on the body until another team arrived. I decided to make some tea after all. I was shaking so badly that it took me three times as long. No way could I measure out loose tea, so tea bags it was.

Cal came into the kitchen.

"Your aim's off. You should've gone to the range like I told you."

"Cal, this is never going to happen again. I don't need a gun. I'm getting rid of it."

"Are you the same person who said she was going into municipal law because she didn't want to see another autopsy report?"

"A fluke. I'm never going to see another autopsy report or have another gun."

"If you're serious about getting rid of your gun, I'll keep it for you."

"Cal, don't keep it for me, I don't want it anymore. I'll give it to you. You can be a walking armory."

I handed him a mug of tea. He looked at it like he wasn't sure he should drink it or not. I poured a dollop of brandy into mine instead of milk. I'd never had it like that before. We toasted, hearing the D.B. team in my living room, talking, moving equipment, walking back and forth past the kitchen door.

The phone rang. Cal handed me the receiver.

"Hello, Jo, I've been calling. You okay?" the familiar voice on the other end of the line asked.

I laughed, but it sounded more hysterical even to my ears. I glanced at the number of messages. Ten.

"I'm...fine. How about you?"

Cal looked away, set his mug down, walked into the hallway, then looked out the front door.

"I've been thinking. I really enjoyed our time together," the voice paused.

"I did, too. Very much."

He spoke slowly, softly. "I wonder if I could see you again?"

"When?"

"Now. Tonight. Had to come back to town. Only have a couple of days here. Dad said he'd talked with you."

Cal came back, picked up his cup. I had the phone in my hand,

187

but put it by my side, and looked at Cal. I could feel the tears were running down my face. I was a freshman again and facing a decision. Deja vu. Cal smiled. Blue eyes, soft, warm. He touched a tear on my cheek with a finger, giving me a slightly puzzled look, but still smiling. I smiled back. I looked at him; he was so easy to love.

So easy.

And now he was getting a divorce and would be free.

I turned my back on him, and put the phone to my ear. "Sure, come on over. There's a bit of a party going on here right now. I'll explain it all when I see you, Sammy."

Photo of Gay Toltl Kinman by Brian and Lilly Loo Studios

Dr. gay toltl kinman coordinates Workshops for Writers at Cal State, San Bernardino, has eight award nominations for her writing including three Agatha Award nominations and has published over one hundred and fifty articles in professional journals. She has published six children's books, several short stories in American and British magazines as well as a gothic novel. Dr. kinman also has had a play produced. In addition she has a recipe included with other famous authors in the book *A Second Helping of Murder*.

Dr. kinman co-edited a cookbook for Sisters in Crime called *Desserticide II* aka *Just Desserts and Deathly Advice* as well as *Shameless Promotion for Brazen Hussies 2*.

For Mystery Writers of America, Dr. kinman has served as Chair of the Edgar Award for Best Children's Mystery and also served on the Edgar Committee for Best Young Adult Mystery. She has been a judge for many contests including original paperback and short story contests for the Private Eye Writers of America's Shamus Awards and also judged the category of short story for the Short Mystery Fiction Society's Derringer Awards. She has also judged several Romance Writers of America contests.

Kinman is a frequent moderator and panelist for Left Coast Crime, Bouchercon, Malice Domestic, Epicon, Mayhem in the Midlands, and other writers' conferences. Also, Kinman is a scholar for the Center for the Book, Library of Congress UCLA "Women of Mystery" discussion group. She is an active member of Mystery Writers of America, Sisters in Crime (former L.A. Chapter Board member), Private Eye Writers of America, Short Mystery Fiction Society, (EPIC) Electronically Published Writers Internet Connection, Women Writing the West, the Dramatists Guild, and the Society of Children's Book Writers and Illustrators.

Kinman has a library degree and a law degree.

To learn more about the author, visit gay toltl kinman's website at http://gaykinman.com

www.ingramcontent.com/pod-product-compliance
Lightning Source LLC
Chambersburg PA
CBHW020409150626
46554CB00012B/444